ONE AND ONE EQUALS MORE

AND FOUR OTHER SHORT STORIES

STEPHANNIE TALLENT

For more information, contact: stephannie@stephannietallent.com

First e-Book edition December 2021

ebook ISBN: 978-1-942655-33-6
Print ISBN: 978-1-942655-34-3

www.stephannietallent.com

CONTENTS

INTRODUCTION

Having read Agatha Christie as a child, I was under the misconception that mystery stories had to include a murder.

They don't.

Welcome to my tenth collection.

Although several of these short stories do have murders, the stories run the gamut from a holiday gone wrong to a woman starting a second career as a penetration security tester.

Stories include the title story, *One Plus One Equals More*; *Saltwater*; *The Final Test of Maria Ramirez*; *Winning The Playa Real Bluffs Holiday Hop*; and *Of Cats and Assassins*.

Enjoy!

SALTWATER

The late morning sky glowed orange through her ash-streaked living room window, backlighting the tall skinny pine trees and thick California oaks that surrounded and shaded her tiny 1940s farmhouse on the north end of Paradise.

A mob of smells assaulted Jenny: woodfire from burning trees and brush, sharp chemical taints from man-made things, the thick stink of petroleum products. Cars, houses, everything.

She could taste the smoke, deep in her throat. She gagged. The thin face mask she wore did nothing to block *anything*, taste or smell.

Her chest ached, breathing hurt, her eyes stung. Too dry to tear up anymore.

And she had to work faster. She thought she could hear a dull roar, the flames rushing closer. She saw a flash up on the ridge to the north. Someone's propane tank? She counted seconds like counting the time between lightning and thunder. One-Mississippi, Two-Mississippi, Three-Mississippi....then the boom from the tank.

Her neighbors, John and Missy, had already fled thirty minutes ago, loading up their quarter horses Fred and Ginger in their trailer, stuffing their golden retrievers Mabel and Rusty into the narrow back seat of their dinged-up but reliable Ford 450. They'd left everything else behind, including John's baby, his vintage 1963 Corvette that he'd restored over the past ten years. He was still working on the brakes. Couldn't trust it, not yet roadworthy.

They had begged Jenny to ride with them.

She couldn't.

Because of *her* baby. Horridly allergic to cats and dogs and everything else with fur, she had instead a 90-gallon saltwater aquarium, a reef tank, her pride and joy. Suited her better anyways as a retired marine biologist than a dog or a cat.

1000 lbs, give or take. Probably give, considering the sand, live rock, and all the filters and other equipment.

Not something she could just pick up and put into her beat up old Geo Metro. Shoot, the aquarium likely weighed more than the damn car.

She'd wrapped the live rock in towels, soaked with aquarium water, and placed it on the back floorboards of the Geo. She saved a little bit of sand, just a cup or two, in a ziplock with more water, and nestled it into the corner of her blue plastic cooler.

The fish and invertebrates went into their own individual ziplocks, with just enough water to give them enough room to turn around and have a little bit of water overhead. A few drops of an ammonia neutralizer. Blennies, Gobis, clown fish. Shrimp.

Fifteen different baggies to cram into the cooler.

She wished she had some oxygen, pure oxygen, to put in the baggies, but she didn't. Smoke-tainted air would have to do.

If she had any moisture left in her eyes, she'd be sobbing. Most people thought fish just swam around and ate and pooped, but she knew each of her fish as individuals. Some were braver, some more timid, regardless of species propensities. Some greeted her eagerly, some were coy, peeking from behind a piece of coral.

Now they were all terrified, and she didn't know how many she was going to lose.

She finally caught them all and got the baggies into the cooler, placing the bottle of ammonia neutralizing drops on top of the baggies. She hoped the cooler would be enough to insulate them, keep their water temperature even.

All she could do is hope.

She lugged the cooler to the Dutch front door, tripping over items she'd tossed around the living room, deciding what to try to bring with her. No to her dive gear, no to her power lifting trophies, no to all her dive and rescue certifications and diplomas, no to anything not essential. In the end, she'd just grabbed a small duffle and stuffed in her laptop and charger, a binder with important papers, a few changes of clothes, and her medication. Last thing she need was a flare up of reflux, and the smoke would only make her asthma worse.

She'd always planned on putting together an emergency kit, especially after the fires in Santa Rosa the previous year.

Planned, never did.

She could see, through the diamond paned windows of the top half of her front door, flickering flames devouring the pine tree tops on the far side of John's sprawling ranch style house against the darkening charcoal sky. A blast of hot air baked her skin as she yanked open the door, picked up the cooler, and ran towards her car.

She tripped over the green garden hose she'd used earlier to wet down the shake shingles of her roof and the painted wooden siding of her house.

She almost dropped the cooler, but juggled it frantically, keeping it upright.

As it was, her right ankle buckled, and she limped the rest of the way to the car. Luckily her car was an automatic, and she could drive with her left foot if she had to.

She careened out of her potholed driveway, tires kicking up gravel, to the two-lane county road.

In her rear-view mirror, she saw embers landing on her roof.

———

11:30 a.m.

If Jenny could just get to Skyway, she might be able to stop at her best friend Arianna Rostler's vet clinic and top off the fishes' bags with oxygen.

As well as seeing if Arianna needed any help with any boarding pets. Jenny couldn't imagine the thought of pets left helpless in kennels and runs with the fire approaching, and she knew Arianna, a well-loved vet in the community for the past twenty years, would never leave them behind. If Jenny could do anything to help, she would.

She'd tried calling Ari from the house with no success; cell service was down. She'd gotten rid of her land line years ago, like everyone else she knew.

She turned southwest onto Skyway. If anything, the smoke was thicker, the sky blacker, and actual fires now dotted the roadside, burning mailbox posts and fence rails. Several buildings had burned to the ground, leaving behind warped skeletons of fallen steel beams on top of heat blasted foundations.

Jenny gripped the steering wheel, nauseated. What if Arianna's clinic was already gone?

It was only a half mile to the Rostler Pet Clinic, but a terrifying half mile, in bumper-to-bumper traffic, moving at a crawl, with the smoke thickening, embers flying overhead, more fire razed buildings on either side of the road. The inside of the Geo was sticky and hot, but Jenny didn't dare turn on the AC, which overtaxed the old radiator even at the best of times.

She finally reached the clinic, a one-story stucco building with runs and kennels behind it. No embers or broken branches burned on the red tiled roof, though the tops of the tall pines shading the runs smoldered.

Arianna's pickup truck, haphazardly backed into the center of the asphalt-paved, six-car parking lot, a half dozen plastic kennels piled in the truck bed, took up most of the small lot. Another car, an old primer-patched blue Honda Accord with a GO BOBCATS bumper sticker, was parked in front the pickup truck, right in front of the main entrance with its double glass doors.

Jenny pulled up on the grass-patched dirt to the left of the driveway.

The front doors were unlocked, but all the lights in the clinic were off. Not much light came in through the front doors or the clerestory windows in the lobby. The sky was too dark.

The clinic smelled surprisingly fresh, lavender essential oil over faint bleach. The electricity must not have gone off too long again. Arianna had installed a top-of-the-line air system; she hated for the clinic to smell like urine or dirty dogs.

But Jenny could also smell a faint coppery odor.

Frantic barks from the rear of the clinic echoed even to the lobby, and she hobbled behind the receptionist's desk as fast as she could on her bad ankle, past the sliding bookcases of manila-folder patient records, to the swinging door that led to the treatment area.

The clinic cat, Mouse, a sweet fat peaches and cream tabby with three legs, two front and one rear, pushed through the door and squeezed past Jenny, nearly tripping her, and ran to the front doors, meowing loudly.

Jenny figured she could catch Mouse on the way out.

She heard a door slam, still ahead of her: the door to the runs out back.

Sprawled on the gray tiled floor of the treatment area was Arianna, in faded jeans ripped at the knees and a ash-smudged Ramones t-shirt, blood oozing from a wound on her left temple, matting her long salt and pepper straight hair.

Oh shit, oh shit. Jenny limped to her, kneeled, and yanked off her face mask. Arianna was breathing, thank god, but she was unconscious. Jenny felt in Arianna's pockets, found the truck keys, put them in her own front pocket, then, still kneeling, grabbed Ari's jeans by her left ankle with her left hand, and lied down perpendicular to Ari, with her back across Ari's chest.

She'd only practiced this maneuver, a Ranger roll, how to get a person on the ground up across your shoulders, while doing ocean rescue training. Never did it in a real-life emergency. But it had to work now.

She couldn't leave Arianna and look for help, thoughts flashing to the burnt-out buildings not even a quarter mile away. She had to get her out of the clinic.

Deep breath.

She rolled towards Ari's head and hoisted herself up at the same time, Ari draped over her shoulders in a fireman's carry. Spikes of pain from her injured ankle left her gasping. She trudged, gritting her teeth, back through the reception area and out to the parking lot.

Mouse, thank god, had hid somewhere. Jenny didn't think Ari would forgive her if Mouse ran outside into the fire and got lost.

The Honda was gone, leaving behind a broken front headlight on Ari's truck.

The strip mall a block over was on fire.

Jenny bent over, balancing Ari, opened the passenger door of the truck, and rotated so Ari would fall into the seat. She buckled Ari in, then limped back to the clinic.

Find Mouse, find the barking dogs, get the hell out. She gave herself five minutes. Any longer and she'd have to leave the animals.

———

Noon.

Mouse huddled in a soft-sided pet carrier between the still-unconscious Ari and Jenny. The cooler of fish and her duffle bag was in the back seat of the pickup, along with a backpack she'd assumed Ari had packed for herself.

Jenny had left the live rock in her now-destroyed Geo. Just not enough time.

Three dogs (a stoic shepherd mix with a bandaged front paw, a little poodly fluffy thing with one soulful dark brown eye and stitches over the other socket, and an irrepressible, just-neutered border collie puppy) occupied carriers in the pickup bed. Jenny had grabbed an armful of old stained donated bath towels, usually used for cage bedding, on her way out of the clinic, and soaked them with water. She'd laid them over the carriers. Not sure if they would help, but she had to try.

The clinic burned behind her. Flames kissed the road. Houses, stores, gas stations (oh, god, what if it explodes as she drives past?), all burning. She couldn't drive fast: other cars clogged the road, and abandoned cars on the roadside, burning debris, and smoke, all the smoke, kept her going slow.

She wasn't religious, but this had to be hell.

She sneezed. Hell with cat fur.

———

2:30 p.m.

She finally reached Highway 99. Ari breathed raggedly next to her, still unconscious. Jenny wished she'd thought to grab a box of surgical masks. Probably wouldn't have helped much with the air pollution, but still.

Hospital. She had to find a hospital for Ari, then police, to report the assault (she shied away from the thought of attempted murder), then find a shelter for the pets, and, finally, for herself and her fish.

———

4:00 p.m.

Jenny pulled into the hospital by the emergency room entrance. The waiting was packed with people hacking, sobbing, whimpering. Other people sat or leaned against the walls, stoically staring at nothing. The still air stank of smoke and fear and disinfectants.

Ari had been rushed back for a CT as soon as Jenny talked to a nurse and told her what happened. Ari had started to stir as Jenny drove into Chico, but still wasn't fully conscious.

The ER staff called the police for Jenny.

"I didn't see anyone," she told Detective Smith, a tall rangy woman in a navy pantsuit, a cream silk tank, and black leather loafers, blonde hair pulled back in a tight low bun, sitting across from her in a quiet corner of the waiting room. "I just heard the door slam as I came into the back room and found Arianna. They had a car, a blue Honda Accord. I didn't think to look at the license plate when I went into the clinic. The car was gone by the time I got Ari out and into her truck."

Smith eyed Jenny's compact, muscular frame. "I think you did an amazing job getting her out. I doubt I'd've been thinking about license plates under the circumstances."

"Ari's truck's headlight is smashed. Wasn't before I went in. Ari babied that truck. Maybe there's some evidence? Paint, something?"

"We'll check. After driving through the fire, though, there might not be anything left." She stood, handed Jenny a business card. "Try the shelter at the Junior High. I think they'll let you keep the critters with you. Call when you get there. I'll send someone to check out her truck. Protocol says impound it, but I can't leave you without transportation, and I want you to get a place to stay before they're all filled."

"Thanks," Jenny said. First priority now was the fish. The only saltwater aquarium store in Chico had closed last year, but she was friends with some of the people who had worked there. Hopefully she could leave her fish with one of them. Then she'd get to the shelter, claim a spot, then hopefully be able to check back in on Arianna. Who knows what she would do about Mouse or the dogs. She didn't know who the dogs belonged to, let alone how to reach them. All Ari's records had burned up.

One hiccupping gasp. She stopped herself from more.

Her house likely gone, her car gone. Her best friend in the hospital with a serious injury, compounded by the time lost between its occurrence and her arrival at the hospital. Her poor fish. Little

Mouse, her home at the clinic gone. The dogs. Who knew if their owners were safe.

Detective Smith reached forward to steady her. "It'll all work out," she said quietly. "You're strong, I can tell your friend is strong."

"Thanks," Jenny said. She just wanted to curl up in a ball on the uncomfortable, worn couch.

But she couldn't. "I'll call you when I get there."

———

6:00 p.m.

Evening. Dark except for the orange glow from the southeast, from Paradise and the surrounding forests and towns. The fish were with Jason, one of the former aquarium store employees and an Afghanistan veteran who was now a biology undergrad at Chico State.

She'd lost several fish, and the rest seemed incredibly stressed, but she trusted him to care for them until she could take them back.

Jason also volunteered to keep the dogs and Mouse for the time being.

"Hey, it's just me and my roomie in this big old house. We have a fenced backyard. I love dogs," he said, rubbing the border collie pup's ear as the pup lounged against his legs.

Jenny almost cried again. But she didn't. She couldn't, yet.

———

6:30 p.m.

She was pulling into the crowded parking lot of the Junior High, and there it was.

The blue Honda Accord, with its GO BOBCATS bumper sticker on a now-damaged rear bumper, dented and hanging haphazardly off the body of the vehicle.

She stared at it. It was definitely the same car.

Cell phone reception wasn't great, but she was able to call the number on Smith's card, fumbling in the faint interior light of the pickup to read it.

"Detective Smith, please," she said. She waited impatiently until Smith picked up.

"The Honda is here," she said. "At the junior high. I'm parking right by it so you can find it." She pulled in behind it, boxing it in. No escape this time.

"Be there in twenty," Detective Smith said, satisfaction apparent in her voice.

Jenny got out of the pickup and followed signs to the gymnasium, limping even more now that she was nearly to safety, no matter how ephemeral. She'd forgot to even mention her ankle at the ER. Well, others had injuries far worse. She was sure she could get some ibuprofen from someone.

Cots were set up in semi-neat rows, with people resting on or around them, what belongings they'd salvaged tucked up under and around the cots. The murmur of conversation, a comforting hum, enveloped her, as did the not-so-pleasant aromas of ash-tinged, stress-filled body odor.

A small group of twenty-something men in stained jeans, dirty t-shirts and scraggly goatees eyed her warily as she trudged past them to the table set up for checking in.

"This one says apomorphine," one of the young men whispered to the other two, examining a translucent orange bottle, half full of small brown pills. "That's morphine, right?"

Jenny forced herself to keep walking, to show no reaction. She knew what apomorphine was. She remembered when Arianna told her about the Schnauzer puppy just this past Halloween, who'd eaten a bag of snack sized chocolate candy bars.

"They're long expired, but they still work," Ari had told her. "Can't get them anymore except from compounding pharmacies. But just a bit of a pill under the eyelid, it gets absorbed, and BOOM! it's like a chocolate Mount St Helens blew up all over the clinic floor."

She cackled, her infectious witchy laugh. "Wrappers and all. Funny thing is, it didn't even smell like vomit. Just melted chocolate. And the poor little pup. She was fine afterwards though."

The banality of evil. Guys who thought it fine to loot a vet clinic for drugs, to assault and leave for dead a woman who had come back to save animals. Jenny stopped before reaching the check in table and redialed Detective Smith.

"I think I found who did it," she whispered when Detective Smith answered. "Three guys talking about apomorphine. It's a veterinary drug." She glanced back. The men had opened the bottle and were passing it around, each palming a couple pills, the last one tossing the now-empty vial onto a blanket covered cot.

"I think it's used in people too," Detective Smith said. "To treat Parkinson's."

"Well, you can make dogs puke with it. I can't imagine why else these guys would have it unless they stole it."

"Just hang tight. We're almost there." Smith hung up.

Jenny limped the rest of the way to the check-in table, and got assigned a cot. The volunteer, a weary woman with dark skin and a short haircut, handed her a small tote bag. "Water, snacks, etc," the volunteer said, her tired voice husky. "As we get more coming in, we'll divvy it up."

"Thanks," said Jenny. "Do you have any ibuprofen? I hurt my ankle."

"Sure do. Let me know if you want me to send any of the medical staff over to check it out," she said, handing Jenny a small foil packet of ibuprofen tablets.

"I'm fine for now," Jenny said.

Jenny passed the three men on her way to her cot. They were whispering excitedly, then each one took the pills they clutched.

Jenny knew, at that moment, her own mean streak was bigger than she would ever admit. She did nothing, nothing to stop them from taking the apomorphine. She didn't know if it would affect them the same way it did dogs, but she was really hoping it did.

She settled on to her own cot, and dry-swallowed four tablets of ibuprofen.

She called the ER to get an update on Ari. While she was on hold, the three men rushed past her towards the back of the gym, to a door labeled Men's Locker Room, clutching their stomachs.

When the nurse told her Ari was awake and asking about Mouse and the boarding dogs, Jenny swallowed a sob. Ari would be fine. Already thinking of everyone else.

Detective Smith and a couple uniformed cops entered the shelter another ten minutes later. Jenny waved, then gestured in the direction of the men's locker room.

"That way," she called, smirking.

Apparently apomorphine *could* affect people the same way.

And when the cops exited the locker room, with miserable hand-cuffed men in tow, and Detective Smith gathered up all the other drugs they'd stolen—ketamine, valium, fentanyl patches, actual morphine—Jenny slumped back on her cot.

And finally, let herself cry, thick salty tears to fill an ocean of aquariums.

THE FINAL TEST OF MARIA RAMIREZ

MARIA TOOK A DEEP BREATH, wishing she hadn't left her travel mug of coffee in her Ford, and licked her lips. If her mouth was any drier it'd be like taking a face plant on the beach and inhaling hot sand.

Nerves. Just nerves.

Face down gangbangers waiting for one of their own, shot and in for emergency surgery? No problem. She'd had nerves of steel as an ER nurse.

She could do this.

Maria ran through her mental checklist: get in, get past the guard, get into the list of rooms she'd memorized. Place the tiny thumb drives in the USB ports of the computers in those rooms. Get out without getting caught.

One last step up to the double glass doors: *Diligence Whitney Federal Building*, fancy black-outlined gold letters stuck to the clear glass.

The 'Y' was peeling at the bottom, dirt caking on the exposed sticky underside.

Time for some housekeeping.

She yanked open one of the glass double doors and marched

straight into the entry hall, orange plastic clipboard in hand. Her no-nonsense white sneakers squeaked against the waxed terrazzo floor tiles.

Metal detector off to her right. Bathroom doors, with an old metal box of a drinking fountain between them, to her left. A government-issue metal desk manned by with heavyset, grizzled older guard in a blue uniform shirt sat between her and the hallway beyond, leading to the banks of elevators and first floor offices.

So far everything looked just like she'd been briefed.

She'd examined the blueprints, too. She liked to be prepared. She always had a good head for spatial relations.

And a certain chutzpah.

The tap of her pen against the clipboard echoed against the nicotine-stained white plaster walls. Her nose twitched. Industrial cleaners. Still couldn't wipe out the stale scent of cigarettes, even though she bet no one had smoked inside for more than twenty years.

And...pastrami and mustard? She eyed the wadded-up brown bag on the corner of the guard's desk. Lunch. She hadn't been able to eat. Too many butterflies.

"Health Department. I'm here for an inspection." Sounded good. Authoritative.

The guard frowned at the boxy beige plastic monitor so old Maria thought the screen would sport neon green characters against a black background. He typed rapidly, then looked up.

"You're not on the list."

"*Random* inspection," Maria said. "Thought this would be a good time to do it, bother the least number of folks, since most are already done for the weekend."

She wore plain canvas khakis, a little tighter on her than she wanted to admit, and a white button down shirt, with black plastic magnetic name tag reading *Maria Morales, Dept Health* stretched over two lines. Her black canvas tote bag hung off one shoulder, the strap indenting her shirt with the weight of her keys and all the thumb drives. It would have been heavier if she'd kept her .45 in its case in there too, but she'd left that in the car.

She couldn't think of any way of smuggling it in, and didn't see why she'd need it, anyways. Even if her boss Jamie at ForgeFire Security told her to keep it with her at all times.

Her straight gray-streaked black hair was pinned up into a messy bun, and her dark brown eyes were magnified by bright red-framed reading glasses.

She looked like an inspector. She knew she did. Middle aged boring woman in a dead-end bureaucratic job.

And she'd chosen today, Good Friday, for her run, because the staff would be limited at the courthouse; and after lunch, because by then, there'd hardly be anyone left at all. Good Friday might not be a federal holiday, but most businesses that kept banker's hours would be shutting down early.

Come on, man.

"I need to call—"

"Then it's not really a random inspection, is it?" Maria asked, stretching up to her full five foot six and leaning just slightly towards the guard, close enough to read his nametag. "*Harold.* And then I have to come back at some time in the future, Harold, and we go through this whole song and dance again."

"What department are you from again?" Harold the guard asked. "Seems like a busy day for inspections."

Maria tapped her nametag. "Department of Health."

"Got any other i.d.?"

¡Dios mío! Of course she'd get someone suspicious. What was Harold, a retired detective? All contract security officers had to have some law enforcement training. Just her luck she didn't get some wet behind the ears kid. She fished out a wallet out of her back pocket, pulled out both a Department of Health i.d. card and business card, and handed them to him.

"There. Happy, Harold?" she asked. "Are you going to let me do my job now?"

Harold the guard examined the card, front and back, then handed it back, along with a lanyard with a laminated orange tag labeled VISITOR OFFICIAL BUSINESS. "Have a good day, Mrs Morales. Through the hallway behind me. Cafeteria is on the second floor, but it's already shut down for the day."

"I've been here before," Maria said. "I know my way around." Granted, that was for one miserable day of jury duty, but Harold didn't have to know that.

Act like you belonged. Act with authority. Jamie had stressed that, time and again.

Easy peasy. She'd run an inner-city ER as a senior nurse before retiring from nursing. This was a piece of cake. She handed her tote and clipboard to Harold (who barely glanced at both) then stepped through the metal detector.

Shoot, maybe she could've gotten the gun in.

"Good to go?" she asked, reaching for her bag and clipboard. "Have a great day, Harold."

"You too, Mrs Morales. Happy Easter."

Maria strode down the hallway, swapping out her *Dept Health* nametag for one that said *Computer Services*. She was in.

Room 110, the office of Assistant District Attorney Sara Roberts, just past the elevators, was her first target.

That name rang a bell, but she couldn't quite place it. She'd been spending more time learning everything Jamie had thrown at her. And then, even though she was on the physical security team, on her own, learning as much as she could about the other divisions in the company. The cyber hacking stuff.

And she had a knack for that, too.

Not important. She had to focus on placing the thumb drives, each preloaded with software that would hack into the hard drives of each individual computer, then migrate out to the main servers. All she had to do was stick them in and kaboom! She earned her paycheck.

Maria jiggled the doorknob on the door to Room 110. Locked.

She squinted through the vintage chicken-wire glass. Couldn't see a damn thing. She knocked firmly, rattling the glass. No answer.

She sighed, then looked around. The hallway was empty, and Harold the guard was seated looking out over the reception area, not looking down the hallway.

Her tote bag had other goodies besides the thumb drives. Maria reached in for her fuzzy bunny's foot key fob with a series of bump keys, her car remote, and her apartment key. She angled her body so that Harold, even if he did look over his shoulder, couldn't see what she was doing, then inserted one of the bump keys into the lock and smacked it with her hairbrush.

The dull thud echoed down the hallway, but Harold didn't even look up.

And just like that, the doorknob turned.

Maria had been appalled when she learned of bump keys. After practicing on the lock on her own apartment front door until she could bump it as fast as just unlocking it, she'd swapped her lock out for a more secure lock, at her own cost.

She bet the courthouse would be installing new locks on the doors after her visit.

She slipped into the quiet office, closing and locking the door behind her. As expected, the office consisted of two rooms: a front area, with a scuffed oak receptionist's desk, and a back room, the door to it shut. The white plaster walls were adorned with artwork left over from the 1970s, bold graphic prints in avocado and gold that fought against the 1920s architecture of the courthouse and the terrazzo tile that extended into the office.

Maria remembered from the blueprints that the back room would have windows overlooking the grass and bushes outside the building. Indeed, a soft afternoon glow lit up the vintage glass of the door leading to the back office.

She turned the knob (unlocked, obviously counting on security of the first door), but didn't open it.

Something felt wrong.

Like she wasn't alone.

And that smell. She knew it from the ER.

She couldn't hear anyone's breath, or even the tiny rustle of clothing, but her instincts were on full alert.

There. The shuffle of steps. The groan of an opening vintage window, then the slam of it shut.

Danger, Will Robinson!

If she didn't open the door, she failed before she even started, and her job as a penetration tester for ForgeFire Security was done. Kaput. Dead.

And Maria wasn't a quitter. She'd raised two kids by herself and put both of them through college, then survived losing both of them in a car crash, all the while working as a nurse til her knees and her back and her soul just couldn't take it.

And learned how to bump locks, after that. Threw herself through crazy obstacle courses. Learned a half dozen ways to kill someone with her bare hands.

Well, maybe not the latter. But she *had* tackled a whole new profession.

She opened the door.

And stifled a scream.

———

Either Sara Roberts hadn't cared about Easter or she had been a workaholic or both, because she was at her desk.

But Roberts wasn't working.

Roberts was dead, dead, dead, a small charred bullet hole centered on her forehead and oh, god, what a mess on the wall behind her, the afternoon light from the flanking windows just putting everything into sharp relief.

Between the nicotine-stained walls in the entry hall and the blood and brain spatter here, the whole damn courthouse needed several coats of paint.

And obviously way better physical security. Who'd Harold let in? An "electrician"? Some other "inspector"? *Busy day for inspectors, huh?*

She stepped up to the desk, hands clasped behind her back, tote bag pushed back so it wouldn't bump forward, to peer at the wound.

Yep. Probably a .45. She'd seen too many wounds like this over the years. So many the smell of gunpowder, urine, and feces smelled like the home that was the ER on a bad night.

A home she'd ran away from as soon as she was able.

A .45. Just like the one Jamie had tried to get her to bring in, but she'd decided against, knowing she had to get past security and the metal detectors. She hadn't trusted coming up with a good story to get out of her bag being looked into.

She had to get out of here. Screw the job.

Maria didn't know if this will all coincidence, her coming in and poor Sara Roberts getting killed at the same time, but she wasn't sticking around.

And besides, her work was unnecessary.

If someone could get in and murder an ADA, then obviously the security sucked.

She backed away from the desk, fishing around for the pack of hand wipes in her tote. She wiped off the doorknob, both inside and out, and tiptoed past the receptionist desk. She was reaching for the doorknob to the hallway when she saw it turn.

"Ms Roberts?" Harold. "Ms Roberts, I got a strange call. I know you said you had a lot of work and to not pester you, but I'm coming in." Keys jangled.

Fuck. Fuckety fuck.

Well, all that time in the gym and doing that damn obstacle course was now useful.

Back to Roberts' office, shutting and locking the inner door. Ignore the dead lady.

The window to the left was locked. Skip it. She'd go out the same window as the murderer. At least she knew that one opened.

The sash-and-pulley windows were likely original to the court-house and just as slow and crotchety as she guessed she would be at the same age. Assuming she made it that long.

She shoved up on both panes, the windowpanes groaning, and squeezed out and let herself fall the four feet down.

Into the rose bushes.

The very, very thorny rose bushes.

Her visitor's tag snagged on one branch. She yanked it off and put it into her tote as she stood up. Her ankle hurt, her face stung, and one palm still had a rose thorn embedded in it.

"Ms Roberts! Oh my god!" Harold's voice, loud enough she thought he was looking down at Maria from the open window.

Maria sprinted.

But not quick enough.

"Mrs Morales! You get back here!"

Maria kept running.

———

Maria had parked her car, a nondescript five-year-old Ford, around the corner from the courthouse, on a eucalyptus-lined street with boxy 1950s houses. She hadn't wanted to mess with the courthouse parking lot with its metered parking and barriers and tickets, even though Jamie had given her a pre-paid parking lot ticket.

Thank god she hadn't.

As soon as she reached her car she scrambled in and went to work.

She unpinned her hair and fluffed it over her shoulders. She took off her red-framed readers and replaced them with aviator sunglasses. Next she pulled off her white button down shirt and balled it up and put it in her tote. Under her shirt she'd worn a tight army green cotton camisole. The day before she'd applied bright floral temporary tattoos, daisies and lilies and zinnias, on both shoulders. The colors gleamed in the afternoon sunlight; they wouldn't really start fading for another few days.

Finally, she swiped on some bright red lipstick.

Not much she could do about the khakis, but if she was driving, and all anyone could see was her head and chest, she looked different enough. She swapped out her utilitarian sneakers for beaded leather flip flops, just in case she had to get out of the car. Her toenails were painted a rich sparkly red—*The Witch's Ruby Slippers*, according to the label.

Maria didn't know if she looked particularly hip, or only like someone too old trying, but she didn't think she looked like a health inspector anymore.

Two patrol cars, lights flashing, screeched past her. One slowed long enough for the cop in the passenger side to take a quick look at her, then it continued to the courthouse.

Maria drove off.

———

Maria didn't head home, to her apartment in Redondo Beach, though that was only about four miles from the courthouse.

She might never go back there.

And she wasn't sure about going to ForgeFire. In fact, she was positive she didn't want to go there.

She turned down Western, towards the 405 freeway. She needed to find a Starbucks or something where she could do some research online.

She'd just gotten onto the northbound ramp when her company cell phone, resting on the dash, buzzed.

She looked at the screen. Jamie.

Fuck. She didn't want to answer it. Didn't want to think, even now, that he might be tracking her with this phone...equipment from ForgeFire.

She lowered the car window and flung it into the weeds next to the on ramp, just missing a homeless man in faded camo pants and a black hoodie. "Sorry, man!"

There was a Starbucks in Westchester. Barely ten miles away but it seemed like more, the other side of LAX. The airport always seemed like a dividing wall along the Santa Monica Bay.

She left the keys in the center console cupholder and put her tote bag in the trunk next to the case holding the .45. She grabbed her messenger bag and personal laptop instead.

ForgeFire had given her a laptop, just like they'd given her a phone. One of the cyber guys explained all the different systems and hardware to her.

This laptop *wasn't* that one.

This was *hers*, purchased with money saved from her first three or four paychecks at ForgeFire (paid training, one of the reasons she'd gone with ForgeFire instead one of their competitors). It was loaded with all the same sorts of software, that she'd purchased on her own. She'd never taken in to ForgeFire for help from one of the guys, not even when she wanted to throw the damn laptop against the wall when she couldn't get things loaded correctly. She'd forced herself to learn it all.

It wasn't paranoia when they might someday be out to get ya, right? The more they'd taught her at ForgeFire, the more cautious she'd become.

Maria pulled out her own personal cell phone and placed a mobile order. The less people she interacted with right now, the better.

The Starbucks was nearly empty, just a few people scattered around drinking lattes or munching on egg bites in between working on their own computers. She picked a table near the bathrooms— and a back exit. She hot-spotted off her phone and ran a search on Sara Roberts while sipping on her mocha. The caffeine settled her nerves.

It didn't take long to figure out why someone would want Sara Roberts dead. Roberts was involved in the prosecution of Mica

Cambridge for running an online fraud and embezzlement scheme—to the tune of millions of dollars.

No wonder Roberts' name sounded familiar.

And Cambridge. Who Maria had met when she first got hired by ForgeFire.

"Hey, Maria, I'd like you to meet my pal Mica," Jamie had said. "Mica, meet Maria Ramirez, one of our most promising new physical security hires. Look at her. She could get in anywhere."

Both men had stepped back, assessing her. Maria knew what they saw: a Latinx woman in her early fifties, dark hair streaked with gray, newly bulked up muscles hidden under a layer of middle age spread. Fine even features in a light brown face: a fading prettiness more forgettable than nondescript.

All of that an *asset*, not a detriment.

Jesus, Maria, how could you be so stupid? She'd been so proud of herself for mastering all the skills required. So proud for studying the blueprints of the federal building for this first real job, she hadn't even thought of the people inside.

Luckily, she had a backup plan. Not just for this job.

For the whole thing. Just in case.

She typed furiously on her keyboard. Then hit return.

Five minutes, and a car marked as an Uber would come get her. And Maria Ramirez—with over two million dollars of ForgeFire's money—would disappear.

Her phone—her phone, her private phone—rang the James Bond theme.

Jamie.

She answered. Four minutes. "Hi, Jamie."

"Maria, honey, what happened? I tried to get you on the phone and it went to voicemail. What's one of the first things I taught you? Never go silent on us. I heard what happened with Roberts. You got out okay, right?"

"I got out fine, Jamie. Just fine." Three minutes.

"Babe, we need you back at the ranch. Are you holding up okay?

Need me to send you a car? I know it can be a real shock, finding a dead body."

"I'm doing fine, Jamie. I've seen my share of dead people, don't you worry." Two minutes. She glanced out the front window. Navy blue Xterra, her contact had said. A CRV drove by. A Forester. And there. She couldn't see through the tinted windows to see the driver, and the angle was wrong to catch the license plate, but how many Xterras were still being driven around?

"Maria. Seriously. Where are you?"

"Jamie, I gotta run. Catch you later, okay?" Maria tapped the hang up icon, then clicked through the steps to reset and erase her phone. She stood and powered down her computer, slid it into the messenger bag.

Maria exited the Starbucks and got into the Xterra.

She'd left the phone on her chair. Maybe one of the baristas would find it. Or another customer. Someone could use it. Treasure it. Not make assumptions.

It was an old model, but it was still useful.

Still had a bit of kick to it.

And a certain chutzpah.

ONE PLUS ONE MAKES MORE

LETTIE SURVEYED the living room of the small shotgun beach cottage, lips pursed. It'd do, she supposed. Clean. Neat. Minimalist, in that short-term rental housing sort of way. Devoid of any personal artifacts.

That was fine by her. The less she had to deal with people, the better.

Hard to avoid people in Pacific Grove, with the tiny cottages just a few feet apart, but winter was the slow season, so there shouldn't be many tourists.

Excluding herself.

Regardless, she knew it would be quiet. Hoped it would be. Just the waves and the foghorns.

She'd have plenty time to relax. Without the fluorescent overhead lights, the constant whirs and clicks and alarms of monitors in the background.

"Oh, Lettie, cheer up." Tia twirled across the bare pine floors, arms up to the white plaster ceiling, like she could reach through it and the Pacific-thick clouds to the pale winter sun above and just pull the sun down to earth, illuminating the shiplap walls and worn floor with limpid dust-sparkled rays. "Can't you smell the ocean? I can even hear the waves. I just love it here."

Lettie could smell the thick ocean brine. Taste it, even, bitter on her tongue. And the pound pound pound of the waves a block away thudded in time with her rising headache. A house this old, built in the 'teens with scrap wood, lacked any insulation against noise or cold.

Scraps of fog from the ocean swirled through the front door, a frail contraption of weathered pine with a nine-paned window taking up the top half. The outside of the door was unpainted, grey wood; the inner was smooth white to match the painted shiplap walls of the cottage. She stepped back to shut it, the old wavy glass shivering in its frame.

The fog seeped in under the ill-fitting door jamb.

Tia ignored the fog, pulling Lettie through the front room with its denim slip-covered loveseat, driftwood coffee table, and blank black TV mounted on the wall, through the dining room with a round oak dining table and two slip-covered, upholstered dining chairs, and into the kitchen.

Lots of slip covers. Easy to keep clean, Lettie assumed.

The kitchen smelled of chlorine scouring powder and lemon countertop spray. It had a white refrigerator, stained porcelain sink (no amount of scouring powder and elbow grease could rid it of the old rust stains), white painted wood cabinets with scalloped trim, and tiled countertops, blue tiles edged with black. The faucet was fitted with a water filter.

A Wedgewood gas stove, all white enamel and shiny chrome, with a blue-faced clock embedded into the back panel, sat opposite the sink. A red tea kettle, enamel chipped, perched on one unlit gas burner.

The scuffed pine floors continued through the kitchen, water and grease stains marking the years of use. *Patina*, Lettie thought, writing a realtor's description. Not old. Not ill-maintained.

"It's so cute!" Tia said, grabbing the kettle to fill it with water for tea. "I love it, I do."

Lettie hadn't noticed the boxes of tea bags on the counter. Tia always noticed the small things. The things that gave her joy.

Of course, that girl found joy in everything. It was a bit wearing.

Tia turned on the stove, listening for the clicks of the igniter. Two clicks, three, then bright blue flames chased around in a circle til the entire burner was lit. She placed the tea kettle back onto the burner, careful to center it just so. She smiled. "Mint tea or chamomile, Lettie?"

"Mint, Tia, thanks." Lettie picked up the box of mint tea, fished out a paper-wrapped tea bag. She sorted through the cabinets til she found a chipped white mug with a logo from the Monterey Bay Aquarium, just to the north a few miles.

"We have to take our meds, Tia," Lettie said after a sip of hot tea, the mint clearing the foggy brininess out of her nose.

Tia slumped. "I'm happy now," she said, the softness in her voice belying her words.

Lettie shrugged. "I'm not," she said. "And you know we promised Dr Smith we'd take them on schedule. We're already late."

They'd skipped the morning meds. Lettie's decision.

Tia didn't question her. She never did.

Lettie reached into her purse, pulled out two bottles. One had ibuprofen, 200 mg per, and she shook out two tablets, then swallowed them, chasing them with tea. She hoped it wasn't too late to stop her headache.

Their headache.

The other bottle... she didn't know quite what was in it, but the little pink and purple capsules pulled her together. Her and Tia. Dr Smith at the Institute for Psychiatric Palliation said it was the only way to keep them functioning. Able to move about in society.

Able to leave the Institute.

Don't ask any questions, and he'd tell them no lies.

She popped one of the colorful capsules and chewed it slowly, waiting for the sparkles to appear.

They did, right on time, illuminating Tia, who was now crying, and Lettie, who dashed at the tears spilling from her eyes.

Then they were *one*, dour Lettie and manic Tia. Just Letitia.

Letitia sighed. Finished her tea. Then explored the rest of the house Lettie had rented for these four weeks.

———

The bedroom was small. No surprise there, given the whole house wasn't more than seven hundred square feet. The full-sized cast iron bed with the plump lichen-colored velvet duvet took up most of it. A side table with a stained glass lamp and a small bowl of lavender potpourri was crammed between the bed and the near wall. An oak armoire was in the far corner, next to the lace-curtained French doors, leading out to the tiny backyard.

The room didn't have a closet. Just the armoire.

Letitia stroked the duvet. Soft.

The bathroom was to the right, with a claw foot tub, pedestal sink, and a water-guzzling toilet. All original, she bet. A window on the back wall, over the toilet, looked out onto the backyard, the glass wavy in its glossy white painted wood frame. Two thick white terry robes hung on a hook on the inside of the door.

The French doors opened up to a wooden deck, two steps leading down to the actual yard. The lower step, a bit soft, creaked. The yard was mostly gravel, with flower beds edging the fence and along the sides of the house and deck. A turquoise blue bistro table and two matching chairs with cheerful bright pink floral cushions (hibiscus, she thought) filled most the deck.

She could picture the blurb:

Wake up in lovely Pacific Grove, cocooned by European linens, and enjoy fresh brewed coffee while wearing one of our luxurious bathrobes on the back patio. Next, take in the salt air breeze during your walk along the ocean-side path, or visit the world-renowned Monterey Bay Aquarium. Let the sound of the waves of the Pacific lull you to sleep at night.

Give Lettie free rein and she delivered, especially since money wasn't much of an issue. It was Lettie's strength, attention to detail and organization way beyond OCD.

As long as she didn't slit her wrists.

Tia, with her butterfly pixie brain, kept Lettie from retracing the silver scars on her wrists.

Letitia wished she could trust Dr Smith. Trust the pink and purple capsules. The meds helped her, they really did. But Lettie didn't trust Dr Smith, and even Tia had her doubts.

We could keep driving, Lettie said.

All the way to LA! said Tia.

"Sorry, guys," Letitia said. "We were driving for four hours. I need a break." They'd taken the coast route from Berkeley to Pacific Grove, stopping for lunch at the Santa Cruz Diner. The Monte Cristo sandwich she'd eaten was the first food she'd eaten in months that tasted *real*, gooey sharp swiss cheese and sweet raspberry jam and salty ham.

The first food in months that lacked a bitter undertaste.

She took one more sip of tea, wrinkled her nose. *That* bitter undertaste.

Dr Smith knew her itinerary. This house that she'd chosen.

That was it. She was going to throw away the tea, the salt, the pepper, anything edible that the house was stocked with. She'd make a note of it all, buy fresh.

She thought of the filter on the faucet.

She'd take it off.

Maybe Lettie was right. Maybe she should just get in her car and drive.

Trackers, kiddo. Lowjack or something like it, said Lettie.

Maybe she'd sell the Honda. Buy a beater. Or just leave it at the

Monterey airport, key in the ignition, and catch a flight somewhere. Anywhere.

She could feel Tia catching her breath. *Really, Letitia? We can finally fly?*

Fly *and* flee. Tia knew that.

Letitia wasn't a prisoner at the Institute. She was a patient.

She could leave anytime she wanted.

As long as Dr Smith okayed it.

———

After unpacking her suitcase (everything meticulously organized in packing cubes, easy to find a place for it all in the armoire), Letitia decided to go to the grocery store. It was already getting close to sundown, and she wanted to get enough items to make herself a small dinner, even if it was just a box of macaroni and cheese and a salad, and some coffee and half and half for the morning. Maybe a loaf of bread and some jam for toast.

She opened the mapping app on her phone. Good. There was a Trader Joe's just a few miles inland.

The cottage had a tiny porch in front, mirroring the back porch. She left the porch light on, then frowned at her car, a silver five-year-old Accord.

Tracking devices?

She felt along the wheel wells. Nothing. Under the front bumper. Nothing.

Under the rear bumper... she felt something. Sharp-edged, an inch by two inches, just a quarter inch high. She tugged. It wouldn't come loose. She could barely fit a fingernail under it.

She kneeled on the road, craned her head sideways. It was too dark to see anything, dusk fast approaching, heralded by the thick fog of marine layer rolling in.

"Need a hand?"

A woman stood on the sidewalk, roller suitcase next to her.

Another tourist, checking into their own shotgun cottage. Snug fitting dark jeans over muscled legs and a cream fisherman's sweater, with her dark hair pulled up in a no-nonsense ponytail. Cool hazel eyes fringed by thick dark lashes.

Letitia glanced to the cottage to the left of hers. Sure enough, the front door was open, and now she was paying attention she could see the shadow of another figure inside, bustling around.

"Dropped my keys," Letitia said, holding them out in one road-smudged hand. "Found 'em."

The woman smiled. "Oh good! Are you here for the weekend?"

"A month," Letitia said shortly.

Don't tell her anything! hissed Lettie.

"Fabulous! We'll be neighbors for a couple weeks. Joe and I are on our pre-honeymoon. We're both high school teachers in Los Angeles, and we're getting married in a month, but school will be in session, so we wanted to get away when we could. I'm Jen." She held out her hand, a big smile on her face.

That smile didn't reach her thick-lashed eyes. Lettie saw that, and so did Tia. *Guys, I know,* Letitia thought.

Letitia waved her dirty hand. "Sorry, dirty, but consider it shook."

"Will do!" Jen said. "Hey, let me know if you want to go to the aquarium. Our rental comes with an aquarium pass. Happy to loan it to you."

None of them, not Lettie or Tia or Letitia, wanted anything to with Jen. Or Joe, who poked his head out of the cottage.

Joe was big and bulky. Letitia bet he coached football as well as taught. He wore dark jeans and a navy ribbed turtleneck and hiking boots.

Did they *try* to match? It was like they were wearing a uniform, Southern California tourists dressing like 55 degrees was 35.

"Need a hand, hon?" he called, then noticed Letitia. "Hi, I'm Joe!"

"Nope, I'll be right in," said Jen. "This is—sorry, I didn't catch your name?"

"Letitia."

"What an old fashioned name!"

Letitia gritted her teeth. Said nothing.

Jen's face tightened, then she smiled. Bright white teeth. "See you later, Lettie!"

———

The cottage was already chilly inside by the time she returned from the store.

She found an electric space heater tucked into one of the lower kitchen cabinets, but decided not to use it. Dinner, bath, bed. She'd just wear one of the thick terry robes over her clothes for now.

Dinner was the whole packet of frozen mac and cheese. The carton said two servings, but maybe that was if it was a side, not a meal. She had to heat it in the stove. There wasn't a microwave.

Might be worth it to just buy a cheap microwave, leave it here for the next tourist. She was going to be here a month.

That is, if she didn't fly, fly away.

Maybe, she thought, drinking a cup of tea (new peppermint tea she'd bought at Trader Joe's, along with fresh filters for the coffee maker, a slew of spices and herbs and other cooking condiments, it was like she was moving in permanently, not just staying a month), maybe, she could trust Dr Smith.

The meds did keep her pulled together. On an even keel. No speed bumps. Smooth sailing.

She took a long hot bubble bath, tossing in bath salts, too. She cracked the bathroom window to let out the steam before climbing in. The water felt silky against her skin. The jasmine bubbles tickled her nose. It'd been so long since she'd taken a bubble bath. Her suite at the Institute was nice, with a big walk-in shower, and plenty of plush towels and eucalyptus and evergreen scented body wash like the spa she used to go to on trips to Santa Fe.

But she missed having a bathtub.

She went to bed early, soon as the bath water had cooled to luke-warm, 9:30 by her watch. An old fashioned time for a young woman with an old fashioned name. She didn't care. This was her vacation.

Her trial period, away from the Institute.

She could hear the waves again, louder, but they weren't pounding against her head like before. Lettie and Tia were quiet. She snugged the velvet duvet up close under her chin and drifted off.

———

Crunch.

Letitia tensed, keeping her eyes closed.

Crunch.

Footfalls on the gravel.

If she kept her eyes closed, no one would be there. No dark shadow beyond the lace curtains.

Crunch.

Then...*creak.* Someone stepping on the lower step of the wooden deck.

She couldn't breathe, couldn't get in any oxygen, though she could feel the pounding of the ocean waves upon the rocky shore, feel her heart thudding frantically against her ribs.

Hold tight, ordered Lettie.

Be brave, whispered Tia.

A soft shuffle-thud, a rubber soled shoe against pressure-treated wood.

The second step.

Another shuffle thud, then a clank and a crash.

One of the bistro chairs?

Shuffle thud, creak, crunch crunch crunch, the crunches fading.

Letitia slipped down off the bed, off the side away from the french doors, then crawled on the floor to the foot of the bed. The pinc floor was icy against her bare knees. Her oversized t-shirt crept up as she moved forward, exposing her lower back. She felt her skin tighten into goose bumps against the cold moist air.

She peered around the end of the bed.

She couldn't see a darn thing.

A foghorn blared and she shrieked.

Nothing. No other noises, until a cricket tentatively chirped.

She hauled herself up using the heavy iron rails of the footboard, then crept to the french doors. She peeked through the lace curtains.

The streetlight out front, dimmed by fog, only cast a bit of light into the backyard.

But it was enough to see that the yard was empty.

And that one chair was lying on its side, floral cushion askew.

———

She twitched fully awake at every heightened noise. Finally, by 6 a.m., she decided to just get up. Pulled on leggings, a sports bra, a long sleeved dri-fit t-shirt, and a red Stanford hoodie. Black running shoes and anklet socks.

She could go for a run on the path that bordered the ocean.

And check under the rear bumper.

She couldn't find a screwdriver or a utility knife anywhere in the kitchen (though she found a drawerful of menus to order takeout, another stocked with takeout containers to use for leftovers, and a drawer with two bottle openers and three different corkscrews) so brought out a butter knife to try to wedge the tracker off.

She crouched down by the rear bumper, running her fingers along the underside.

And did it again.

And once more.

Nothing.

The tracker was gone. She lay nearly flat on the damp road, craning her neck to look. To be sure.

"Dropped your keys again?"

Letitia banged her head on the bumper, then clambered up, rubbing the back of her head. That *hurt*. She could feel a headache barreling in.

Take some ibuprofen, Tia said.

Before you go on the run, said Lettie. *Use it as an excuse to get away from these two.*

Joe and Jen stood just a few feet away, both in their uniform of jeans and sweaters (hers navy, his cream, this morning), and heavy khaki canvas jackets with hoods. Jen wore knitted fingerless mittens. They both smiled, teeth white and shiny, but their eyes were shark dead.

"Nah. Someone dinged me in the Trader Joe's parking lot last night, just couldn't see if there was any damage then. It's a busy cramped lot, be careful if you go." Letitia popped up to her feet, knees twinging. "Bumper looks fine though."

Please don't lie to me, Ms Brown, said Dr Smith. *I can always tell when patients lie, and it doesn't go well. How can I ever trust you if I know you're a liar?*

"But ouch. I'm going to grab a couple ibuprofen before my run." Letitia walked back into her house, legs shaky. She had too many voices in her head right now. Lettie and Tia, she could deal with. They could even be useful. But she needed to never hear Dr Smith again. Never.

She popped three ibuprofen and one pink and purple capsule.

She took off all her clothes and pinched her fingers around every seam. Everything felt flat. Nothing implanted. No trackers.

She felt all over her backpack, but the seams were too irregular to tell if there was anything there. She sat it aside.

Three hundred dollars cash in her wallet.

That wasn't enough.

The minute she tried getting cash back on any of her credit cards she was sure Dr Smith would find out. Same with going to a bank and making a withdrawal, but she had to risk it. She'd checked before she left the Institute; there was a branch of her bank in downtown Pacific Grove.

She couldn't take her car. Just because one tracker was removed, didn't mean there weren't others, trickier to find.

And her phone. She was sure he could track her by her phone.

Go for a run to kill time and look normal. Have a good breakfast. Pack a lunch.

Maybe even go to the Aquarium. Act normal. She could buy some extra clothes at the gift shop. Even buy a backpack. Pay cash.

Hit the bank on the way back from the Aquarium. Withdraw every bit of money from her savings account. If she could just get enough cash for a laptop, she would be set.

And she could fly.

———

The Aquarium opened at 9 a.m. Letitia was there, head of the line at 8:55, poised to rush the door, pretending to read the brochure and map.

"Hi there! I told you we had passes, you should've let us know you were coming here today!"

Letitia turned, toast-filled tummy suddenly hollow.

Jen stood there, shark teeth grinning. Joe loomed behind her.

"Would you like to explore the aquarium together?" Jen asked.

"Sorry, no," Letitia said.

Get the fuck out of here, Lettie whispered. *They know.*

They know, Tia said. *Run, Letitia. Run.*

Liars don't get any special privileges, Dr Smith said. *No matter the size of their trust fund.*

"Get out of my head," Letitia whispered.

"Did you say something, hon?" Joe asked, his tone concerned and his blue eyes cold.

"No," Letitia said. "I have nothing to say to you."

The doors opened and she pushed through, giving her ticket to the docent.

She wandered through the different exhibits. She could always feel Joe and Jen around her, watching her, even when she couldn't spot them. She tried to enjoy the sea otters, the big tank of the local fish, calico bass and bright orange Garibaldi.

Long ago, ten years ago when she was doing her undergrad at Stanford, she dabbled in Marine Biology, before making her parents happy and settling into Computer Science. BB. Before Breakdown. BA. Before Accident. BS. Before Scars.

She'd visited at least each exhibit once and the sea otters twice before hitting the gift shop.

Normal people bought souvenirs.

She bought a backpack, black with the aquarium logo in light blue; a gray sweatshirt featuring a baby sea otter; a black tank top with a school of jellyfish; and gray sweatpants with black racing straps up the sides and a small aquarium logo on the back waistband. A denim baseball cap with an octopus embroidered on it, the tentacles extending along the brim.

Any additional clothes and she feared it would be too suspicious. The pants were pushing it.

Everything fit in a large paper bag. She felt bad about the bag, especially when the cashier, a cheerful young woman (KATHY said her name tag), gave a polite but pointed look at her new backpack.

She spotted Joe and Jen on her way out of the Aquarium. Rather than heading right, down the ocean-adjacent path back to Pacific Grove, she turned left to the tourist district, and ducked into one of the restaurants (LOCAL ABALONE! FISH! CHOWDER!). Just a thin thirty-something woman with scared green eyes, pale skin, and mousy hair caught up in a loose bun at the nape of her neck, exploring the town.

"Bathroom?" she asked, barely waiting for directions. The thick odor of fried fish cloyed.

Rather than go into the ladies' room, she continued straight down the hallway, past the bustling, clanking kitchen, and into a small alleyway. She went through the first open door she found, the back door into yet another restaurant, the air thick was stale cooking oil, and ducked into a gender-neutral, one-person bathroom. She balled up the paper bag, stuffing it deep into the trash can, and shucked off her clothes, all but her plain cotton bra and panties, pulling on the aquarium sweats and tank top. She unpinned her hair, shaking it into loose waves, and plopped on the cap.

Cute, breathed Tia.

Lettie snorted.

She was as different as she could make herself. She hefted her leggings, t-shirt, and sweatshirt.

They *seemed* safe.

She pulled out the paper bag from the trash and stuffed the sweatshirt, t-shirt, and leggings into the trash, then placed the bag on top of the clothes. She moistened and balled up a dozen paper towels and tossed them in, too.

She walked out the front door, up one of the side streets, and back south towards Pacific Grove.

After about a half mile, she started jogging.

She didn't see Joe and Jen.

———

She had to go inside the bank. All she'd kept out of her wallet was her license and a small, laminated copy of her SSN card. No ATM card, no credit or debit cards.

This is stupid, groused Lettie. *Where else do you think they'll guess you'll go?*

Be careful, Tia warned.

Letitia dry swallowed another one of those little pink capsules. Lettie and Tia faded.

$2000 was safe.

$10,000 was the absolute most she could get at one go, and even that depended on who she talked to. $10,000 would attract attention. Way too much attention.

But $2000 wasn't enough.

If you're asking for more than two, you might as well as for ten, Lettie interjected.

She was right. Lettie usually was.

Of course, Lettie was the one with a death wish.

"I'd like to withdraw two thousand from this account," Letitia said to the teller, a nice young man named Kit. "Five hundred in twenties, then the rest as hundreds."

Who named their kid Kit? He was too old for Game of Thrones fan parents.

Kit. Kathy. Who next? Katie, Cat, whatever? Were they all plants? Was this all a set up?

Maybe, whispered Lettie.

Just because you're paranoid doesn't mean we're not all out to get you, my dear, said Dr Smith. *Check in with Joe just outside. He's waiting for you. Pissed off because you ditched them in Monterey.*

Kit passed the money to her. She stuffed it all into her backpack, ignoring his raised eyebrows.

"Do you have a restroom I can use?" she asked.

"Back hallway," he said.

Of course. Down the hallway. Past the bathroom. Out through the emergency exit.

Ow, Tia said. *The alarm hurts my ears.*

Run, kiddo, Lettie added.

She sprinted north. Main Street was really the main street of Pacific Grove. The streets paralleling it were semi-residential, featuring some of the bougainvillea-fronted, nineteen-teens cottages like her rental, interspersed with antique shops and law offices. One block, two blocks, three. She turned right on the next side street, and got back on Main Street.

There. A taxi, a Prius, adrift in a sea of Lyft and Uber stickered cars, its lime green paint job like a flashing neon sign. She flagged it down. Watched it pull out towards her.

And cried out when Jen grabbed her arm, pinching her cruelly.

"Where do you think you're going?" Jen hissed, hauling Letitia away from the curb.

Joe was striding down the street towards them.

The taxi was pulling up, its gray-haired, pony-tailed driver with a bewildered look on his face.

FIGHT! screamed Tia.

FIGHT, you idiot! yelled Lettie.

Letitia hauled back and threw a wild punch. A lucky punch.

She hit Jen's nose, knocking it sideways. Blood gushed out and Jen dropped into Letitia's arms, both hands reflexively covering her nose.

Joe broke into a run.

And Letitia dove into the back seat of the taxi.

"Go, go, go!"

———

"Where you heading, kiddo?" the driver asked. He was heading south on the 101, towards Carmel. Towards the exit for the Monterey regional airport.

Right where they'd expect her to go.

"San Jose?" she asked timidly.

"Where do you *need* to go?" he asked, one bushy gray eyebrow raised up. She could see his face in the rear-view mirror. He looked kind, his face craggy with age and hard living. Deep laugh lines bracketed his mouth.

Dr Smith looked kind, too. But his face was round and squishy. Soft.

Trust, whispered Tia.

No other choice, said Lettie.

"Away. Far away."

"I go to Las Vegas once every few months since the missus passed. That sound good?"

Letitia cleaned back against the seat, rubbing her right hand. Hitting someone hurt. Her knuckles were already swelling up. "Stop at an Apple Store in Bakersfield? I have to buy a computer."

"Will do, hon. We'll get gas in Bakersfield too. These hybrids get good mileage. That should get us to Vegas."

Sounds like a plan, Lettie said.

Fly, Letitia, fly, murmured Tia.

"My name's Reggie," the cabbie said.

Letitia pressed the button to roll down the rear window. Tossed out the pink and purple capsules. Watched the amber vial bounce on the highway, then into the tall brown grasses.

"Thank you. My name's Letitia. But you can call me Lettie. Or Tia."

OF CATS AND ASSASSINS

MAGGIE FIDGETED at the white and gray marble bar, sandalled feet dangling off the industrial chic leather and steel barstool. She inhaled the sharp citrus smells as the barkeep, a trim man dressed in black trousers and a blindingly white pressed shirt with a bolo tie with a hunk of turquoise, cut lemons, limes, and oranges. Prepping for the hotel happy hour rush.

The other barkeep, a woman dressed nearly the same as the man (with an orange and brown agate on her bolo tie, not a turquoise), washed up some glasses from lunch, the tinkle of glassware providing just enough background noise to keep Maggie from exploding with pent up energy.

Maggie was set up just so, on her barstool; she could see the tall glass front doors opening into the hotel lobby if she glanced to her left in the mirror mounted on the wall behind the bar, and she could see, by looking to the right in the mirror, anyone entering the bar itself.

She already could describe everyone in the bar. The errant curly gray hairs poking out of the elderly gentleman's ears, sitting in the last booth to her left, shrouded in darkness, drinking his third whiskey since she'd come in a half hour before. The young couple sitting at the high top to her right, chatting excitedly about what bands they'd go see on 6th Street that night, each drinking local craft brews (a stout and a hazy IPA). The waitress just starting her shift, dressed in a black cocktail dress and low-heeled black pumps, her eyes already tired. The group of businessmen in the big round booth, discussing their plans for the InnoTech conference tomorrow, sharing a pitcher of light beer.

She had to sit up straight to lean her elbows on the cold marble, sit up straight with posture that would make her old West Point classmates proud. Doing so stretched out muscles achy from last night's job in Dallas. Scaling the side of a building, even with proper equipment, took a fair amount of upper body strength. Maggie's childhood training as a gymnast served her well.

She hadn't expected another job so soon. Usually she went weeks, months even, between assignments, enjoying her time off on lounging a sandy tropical beach with cerulean waters, or skiing in the granite peaks of the Dolomites, or even just sauntering down the streets of Paris, shopping for trinkets at the antique markets for an apartment she rarely lived in.

Alone, always alone, but she'd never met anyone who could match the adrenaline of her work.

But this was the third job in two weeks. She'd gotten the text late last night, with concise instructions. Get to Austin first thing in the morning. Check in at the Old Congress Avenue Hotel under the name Megan Knight. Await further orders.

They'd tossed in a nugget of intel: the target had booked the three adjacent suites and would be checking in prior to her arrival in Austin.

She'd just finished cleaning up from the Dallas job, damn it.

No doubt the company knew that. She supposed she should be grateful they let her wash the blood out of her hair.

Just—she was *tired.* Damn it.

She was paid well for the work she did. She couldn't say she truly enjoyed it, but it was a necessary job, and she was quite good at it. If she lived long enough, she had no doubt she'd be the best, one day.

Her cell phone, sitting on the counter in front of her, vibrated and played the outer space theremin tune. She accessed the document it heralded.

She wondered who she'd have to kill this time.

———

Simon watched the woman from, he'd determined, the only spot she didn't have covered with a direct or indirect line of sight.

He slumped in a deep leather armchair in the hotel lobby, newspaper spread out on the low marble-topped table in front of him, open laptop browser opened to various stock analysis sites. Camouflage.

She was clever, but so was he. And he had the benefit of knowing what his target looked like. She had no idea he even existed.

Two men had died, putting together the packet on Maggie Justin. He didn't intend on squandering their sacrifice.

Her target this time, a last minute assignment, was Kostya Andreevich.

Andreevich was an evil person. Simon couldn't argue that. But Simon's employers apparently found Andreevich useful at this moment in time. Simon's job was to foil Maggie. In any and every way necessary.

Pity. She was attractive, bigger than life, all that energy packed into a tight muscular five foot frame. Sun-lightened brunette hair flowed from a neat ponytail down her back. He couldn't see them, but he knew from photos that her eyes were blue flecked with gold, ringed with dark thick lashes.

She wore a sleeveless sundress, printed with daisies, and strappy high heeled sandals. A distressed denim jacket dangled off the back of her barstool. The dress suited someone ten years younger than her thirty three years, but she pulled it off. She looked young and innocent, and he was sure that was her intent.

He wished he didn't find her so very attractive. Not just her physical self, but the daring and cleverness that was revealed in the packet he'd reviewed just the other day.

West Point graduate, five years in military intelligence, but also one of the few women selected for, and who graduated from, Ranger School. Service in the Mid East, including medals for bravery under fire. That intel was easy to find. All public record; some it, the Ranger School selection and graduation, *very* public, though she let her classmates have the limelight best as she could.

Then things got interesting.

After leaving the military, she'd been hired into a paramilitary firm, worked through their training courses, and deployed to various locations, primarily doing bodyguard work for the wives of high ranking officials.

A year of that, and she get earmarked for even more specialized training: spy craft and assassin training.

Oh, the firm wouldn't call it the latter. In fact, this was some of the intel that cost Davey Roberts his life. That section of the firm was totally black, totally hidden, and the list attained by Davey, of graduates (not just Maggie) and their skills, would pay off for years.

Roberts had identified a list of at least twenty jobs to which she'd been assigned. Assassinations. He'd died in a car wreck, deemed an accident by Simon's employers, but Simon wasn't so sure.

No five foot-tall brunettes were anywhere near the site of the accident. That didn't mean her firm hadn't caused the accident.

He'd never met a woman like her before.

————

Maggie ordered a Manhattan. Up, no ice. Two cherries, not the neon pink travesties, but the deep dark rich ones. She had the feeling she'd need a real drink after reading her assignment, not the sparkling water she'd been nursing.

She snagged a compact out of her purse, a tan leather satchel that held all sorts of interesting toys. Nothing, of course, was what it appeared. Well, the hotel key card was just that. But everything of *hers* had multiple uses.

The mirror on the compact sharpened and magnified objects, for example. And if she slanted it just so (meanwhile swiping on some vanilla mint lip balm that also served as a very good lubricant for recalcitrant door locks), and angled the compact so she could see the side mirror in it, she could glance at her one blind spot every so often.

Same guy who'd been sitting in the dark brown club chair, with a newspaper and his laptop. Mid thirties, she guessed, with dark brown hair already silvering at the temples. Boyish, with dimples and a mouth meant for broad smiles. Snug dark jeans, brand new ostrich skin cowboy boots, chambray shirt, and a navy blue wool blazer stretched across broad shoulders.

Cute.

Really cute, actually.

Really, *really* cute.

And, she told herself, *suspicious*, just because of his presence here. Because he was sitting in her blind spot, in the lightly populated hotel lobby. He could be here for that InnoTech conference. He looked the part, though underneath the Austin business casual clothes his body seemed muscular, not pudgy like the guys at the bar table.

He could have a perfectly innocuous reason for having chosen that seat.

Other than it was the best one to observe her from.

She didn't trust coincidence.

Too bad, because a diversion would be nice, after the job.

She started reading the assignment, phone held close in hand, Manhattan in the other.

Her knuckles whitened.

———

Simon saw her go rigid, then jump off the bar stool and head towards the bathrooms.

Something had rattled her. A woman he thought unflappable.

Follow? Not follow? He packed up his laptop, leaving the newspaper scattered, then headed for the men's room.

———

Maggie locked the door of the ladies' bathroom after making sure no one was in any of the stalls. She leaned against the vanity, marbled topped walnut. A basket of folded cloth towels sat next to the basin, and a wicker basket on the floor collected the used towels. She could smell the soap and hand lotion, dispensed from pseudo-vintage-labeled brown bottles. Rose hips and sandalwood. Fancy. All of it: the lotion, the cloth towels. It suited the renovated historic hotel.

She wanted to gag.

She punched in a number from memory, though she'd never actually called it before. Never had to call it.

"You're kidding, right?" she hissed into her phone. "I can't do this. I won't."

She listened for a moment. "They were all bad people," she said. "You promised, you'd never have me go after an innocent."

A few more moments.

"I don't care how much you pay me. Assign me *him*, Kostya Andreevich, I'm fine with that, I know what he's done," she said.

"But not his *cat*." She disconnected, trembling, then left the bathroom.

———

Simon reached the hallway to the bar bathrooms just as Maggie left the ladies' room.

He stopped before he could run into her, reaching out to the dark wallpapered wall to stop his momentum, his messenger bag with his laptop thudding against the wall as well.

Her eyes were bluer than the photo, the glints of gold brighter, even in the darkness of the short hallway, even with him blocking most of the light from the bar. Her mouth was set in a thin line, so different than the photos showing her laughing, talking. Those remarkable eyes narrowed to match her mouth.

"Excuse me," she said, her voice steel wrapped in velvet, a rough burr that zapped his spine.

"So sorry," he said, stepping aside to let her past. She stalked past, brushing against him in the narrow hallway. Electric zaps this time, turned up to eleven. *Play it cool, old chum.* He didn't even turn to watch her walk away, just barged into the men's room. He washed his hands (nice, rose and sandalwood), dried them, left.

What had gotten her knickers into a twist?

———

Australian, Maggie guessed, from the accent.

And even more handsome up close.

She'd stuck a tiny transponder onto his jacket as she'd passed him. It looked like a piece of lint. She hoped he wouldn't notice it. If he was there to watch her (or, even worse, interfere), she'd find out.

While figuring out what to do about her assignment.

What were they *thinking*? She loved cats. She could never hurt one. And they wanted her to go all horse head Godfather on it?

She'd take the cat. She'd take it, and keep it herself, so no one else could complete the assignment.

She could find something gruesome that would serve the same sort of warning.

We're watching you. We can get to you, anywhere.

She'd passed plenty of road kill armadillo driving from Dallas to Austin. A couple of those would certainly send a message.

She grabbed her jacket from the back of her barstool, quaffed the rest of her Manhattan, and headed to the elevator to her room.

———

She didn't travel cheap, Simon thought, watching her enter the penthouse elevator.

"Any penthouses left?" he asked the desk clerk, a young Asian woman with raspberry colored hair and red rose tattoos on her forearms, trailing up under the sleeves of her crisp white blouse.

One of the penthouse suites was available.

"Last minute cancellation," she told him. "The man who booked three suites decided he just needed two."

"I hope it's not some big party situation," he said. "I have work to do. Conference tomorrow."

"It's all soundproofed," she assured him. "And they don't seem like the partying type. Two men, one with a cat, of all things. But we've seen worse," she said, leaning towards him. "We had one group that brought their emotional support pot bellied pig."

"The other party in the other suite?"

"Just a woman here for work as well," she said.

Someday, some operative was going to take care of this chatterbox just out of general principles. "I'll take it."

———

Maggie didn't know if the penthouse suite itself was worth the price, but the location, next to the three suites the target had booked, made it worth it — at least to her firm, who'd booked it for her.

It took a team to set up these assignments. She was just the bullet of the gun.

The suite was roomy, with a bedroom area and an ensuite bath to the right, a powder room to her left, and a big living room with a limestone fireplace directly through the entrance. It smelled fresh, a hint of eucalyptus. Spa-like. The cream colored carpet was plush, hushing her footsteps as she crossed the living room. She gave into temptation, kicking off her sandals and curling her toes into the carpet, stretching out her feet.

Abig oak desk, with plenty of plugs and ports for her laptop, and a comfy, cognac leather office chair, filled the far end of the living room. Eames soft pad executive chair. She suspected the chair was not a replica.

The desk overlooked the Austin skyline to the south. The Colorado river glinted in the late afternoon sunlight. She might get a view of the famous bats leaving the Congress Avenue bridge at dusk, spiraling into the air, even.

A bottle of sparkling water on a leather coaster sat on the desk, along with a pen and a pad of paper. She opened the water, guzzled it, and placed the pen and paper into the uppermost desk drawer, before setting up her laptop.

Maggie transferred the packet from her phone to her laptop. She opened the zip drive, scanned the folders, and clicked on the one for the hotel itself, then the file for the architectural drawings of the top floor.

The hotel was old, built at the end of the 1800s, of Burnet County red granite and Hill Country limestone. It had been derelict, abandoned, only twenty years ago, before being purchased and renovated. The plans she had included all the foibles of the original construction as well as the updates from the renovation.

She wasn't surprised Kostya Andreevich had chosen this hotel. It was expensive, though not flashy, and would impress his clients with both the cost and his taste. Three suites. One for him, one for his bodyguards. What about the cat that apparently travelled everywhere with him? It got a suite, too?

Nah. The cat, according to the file, slept with him, on his pillow.

She'd have to get into his suite, and unfortunately, that meant either through the front door or one of the windows. There wasn't any sort of ventilation ducts or anything like that large enough for a person. There was a small attic-like floor above theirs, insulation and some ducts and wiring and so on, but it was only accessible via the interior staircase adjacent to the elevator.

There was also the issue of *which* suite.

She had an array of small cameras she had set up when she first checked into the suite to monitor the doors, knowing that her target would be occupying one of those suites. There'd been no time to get into the suites themselves, to set up cameras inside. The target had checked in earlier that morning, while she was still on the road from Dallas. She checked the feed from the cameras to her laptop.

Static.

She swore softly. She'd have to check the cameras.

Padding across the room, she stopped at the front door. Peeked through the peep hole. No one was outside, and the elevator floor indicator light showed it was on the ground floor.

She slipped outside into the marble floored foyer. Each suite occupied one corner of the top floor, and the elevator and foyer took up a small bit of space in the center. She had placed cameras, tucked up under the molding on the walls, such that she could see each doorway.

The elevator pinged just as she was reaching, tippy toes, for the first camera, located under the molding above the elevator. The floor indicator light still showed the elevator was on the first floor as the door opened.

Aussie guy stared at her.

Up close she could see his eyes, dark hazel fringed by thick lashes, like a sun-dapple forest creek, back in Georgia during her Ranger training. A little bit of 5 o'clock stubble along his firm jaw and dimpled chin, just highlighting the angles, inviting her caress. That bit of silver at his temples, imparting just enough age and experience.

She'd never reacted to anyone like this before, never, and certainly not someone with a nefarious purpose. She knew, with every bit of her training and experience, that he was not on this elevator, exiting onto this floor, by accident. He was either there for Andreevich or for her. Given he'd been watching her from the lobby, that he followed her to the bathrooms, she knew what the answer was.

And, close enough to kiss him, she flat out didn't care.

Until her professionalism kicked in.

"Excuse me," she muttered, pushing past him onto the elevator. Someone just waiting for the elevator, caught in an awkward pose.

"You're going downstairs without your shoes?" he asked in that adorable accent. He followed her back into the elevator, blocking her exit.

Sure, she could get past him, but that would reveal her skills more than the mishap with her sandals.

"I just need to get something from the front desk," she said, jabbing the lobby button on the vintage panel.

"Phone doesn't work?" he asked as the door slid closed.

The elevator was small, with a beveled mirror just on the back wall. Worn oak paneled the rest of the walls, in keeping with the hotel decor. Used only by the penthouse guests, it smelled faintly of expensive cologne from previous occupants, cedar and musk, lightly enough to be interesting, not cloying.

His presence, on the other hand, permeated the elevator. She didn't have anywhere to go. She pressed herself against the mirror, heart pounding despite herself, claustrophobia and adrenaline both kicking in. *Breathe, Maggie. Breathe.*

"My name's Simon," he said. "You're Maggie, right?"

———

There she was, one arm stretched up, on her tiptoes, reaching above the edge of the elevator. She was still in her daisy-splattered sundress, backlit from the foyer lights, but barefoot. Simon inhaled sharply.

"Excuse me," she said, nearly knocking him over as she entered the elevator. Just that brief touch zapped his spine again. She was close enough to kiss, for him to wrap his arms around her and nestle her against him.

"You're going downstairs without your shoes?" he asked. He couldn't think of anything else to say, but he had to say something.

"I just need to get something from the front desk," she said, daring him to challenge her.

So he did. "Phone doesn't work?"

She pressed against the back of the elevator as the car moved down, not replying.

He almost, almost reached out to her, but said, "My name's Simon."

She didn't reply.

"You're Maggie, right?"

Those magical blue and gold eyes met his. "And you," she said precisely, "are dead."

Quick as a striking tiger snake she launched herself at him, a flurry of kicks and punches that he could barely match. She struck at his nose, and shooting pain staggered him even as he whipped his head back. Spots in front of his eyes. She viciously kneed towards his groin (a diversion, thank god) while punching at his throat. He dodged *that*, then went on the offensive.

Given more room to dart and retreat, or if she'd been armed, even with a pocket knife, he had no doubt she could've destroyed him, she was that fast.

But she didn't have room to maneuver, and he finally pinned her against his chest, one arm across her throat, the other around her chest and arms. She struggled briefly, then slumped.

He didn't relax his hold.

"I don't want to hurt you," he whispered. "I just can't let you do whatever you're supposed to do."

"You know what I'm supposed to do?" she said, quivering against him.

She snorted.

Laughter. She was *laughing*.

"I'm supposed to kill and skin his damn cat and arrange it on his pillow," she said.

"You're kidding. That's disgusting. And inhumane. You're not here to kill Andreevich?"

"Nope. Not that he doesn't deserve it."

He agreed with her on that. Kostya Andreevich mined and sold data on sensitive material. Didn't sound that bad until you realized that information was the keystone for toppling corporations and even governments, available to the highest bidder regardless of morality or ethical considerations, or what might happen to people afterwards. And he didn't always take money as payment. Simon had heard about women and girls disappearing after being given to Andreevich.

"My company just wants to remind Andreevich that no one is untouchable."

"And they want you to kill his cat." He bent his head to her hair. Coconut and sea salt. Smelled like the beach, her shampoo did. Made him yearn for his surfboard.

"Apparently he loves that cat more than anything else in the world." She shrugged, still contained by his arms, not fighting. "I'm not going to. I can't. I'd happily kill him, but I can't kill an innocent cat."

"What if it scratched you and bit you?" he asked, lips just above her hair. "Would you still feel that way? Could you forgive it, and still save it?"

"A cat is a cat. If it's scared, or threatened, it'll attack. Or run," she continued, voice softening. "It's only reacting as you should expect." She twisted in his arms, just enough to look up at him, her gold-flecked eyes deepening to indigo.

God, she was sexy.

"You save the cat. We'll think of some other message. I'll help you, kitten," he said. "That way we're both following orders."

And the elevator door pinged.

———

The lobby. Simon released her, and both were facing the elevator door as it opened. She snuck a quick look at him. Both of his eyes were already blackening, and a trickle of blood stained his upper lip. His nose was swollen.

"Blood," she said. "Upper lip." Part of her, the feral side, wanted to jump up, wrap her legs around his waist, and lick that blood off before kissing him.

"Got a tissue, kitten?" he asked.

She snorted. "I left the room without shoes. You see a purse anywhere?"

He grabbed her arm before she could step out of the elevator.

She let him.

"Let's just go back upstairs," he said. "We have a mission to plan, don't we?"

She tapped her keycard against the reader and punched the button for the penthouse level. "I'll get room service to get a bag of frozen peas for you."

"Charge it to my suite," he said.

"You're up here too?"

"Your target cancelled his third suite. I got it," he said. "P2."

"I'm P1." Lucky she hadn't tried to break into the suites, then. She'd've tried his, adjacent to hers, first.

"What were you going after above the elevators?" he asked as the elevator zipped up.

"Cameras. They fuzzed out. I wanted to check them. I'm not sloppy," she said. "The elevator light said it was on the ground floor. I couldn't hear it until the door opened."

"I wouldn't dare think you were sloppy."

She grinned and tugged at his left arm, then held up the tracker. "Not sure you're not," she said.

"Bloody hell—" he said, then remembered. "The hallway by the bathroom. You bumped me."

"Bingo," she said, as the elevator door opened up once more.

———

Andreevich stood right in front of the elevator, a bodyguard to either side.

He was of average height and build, with lustrous dark hair pulled back into a long ponytail. He wore a simple but well-cut black suit, blue and white striped shirt, and a dark blue tie. Nothing flashy, except one chunky gold ring, studded with diamonds and aquamarines, on his right-hand ring finger.

His long blue-black hair was the only thing that stood out. Well, that, the dead shark look in his black eyes, and the cream colored cat hair scattered across his shoulders.

"Darling, let's get to our room, shall we?" Simon said, tugging her along.

They walked around the silent Russian to Simon's suite, not waiting to hear the elevator door close before entering. Simon gestured to her, letting her enter first.

The suite was a mirror image to hers, though the view wasn't as good, looking to the west and north rather than the west and south. He would, though, get a glimpse of the State Capitol. She padded to the window. It was getting close to dusk.

"You can see the bats from my windows," she started, then he wrapped his arms around her, pulled her back against him.

"I'm interested in *you*," he said. "Not the bats, not Andreevich, you. He's probably going to dinner. Or a meeting. Give him ten minutes to make sure he's not forgotten anything, then we'll go in. Get the cat. Get out."

She twisted in his arms and wrapped one leg around his, pulling him closer, then stretched up. He wasn't terribly tall, about five-eleven, but he towered over her. He scooped her up, letting her wrap her legs around his waist. She didn't care that her dress was hiked up. All she cared about was his lips, so close to hers.

"You don't have any claws you're going to stab me with, do you, kitten?" he asked.

"Would I tell you?" She could feel him, hard against her, and she sighed.

He lowered his head just a bit more, nipped at her lower lip. She grabbed the nape of his neck and kissed him, tentative at first, then with more force, tasting him, letting him taste her, then pulled back.

"Ten minutes?" she said.

"We'll give him more time than that," he said, shuffling over to the bedroom door, still holding her against him. "You can be patient, right?"

She stared into his hazel eyes. "Yes," she whispered.

She thought she'd waited her whole life to meet someone like him.

———

She watched as he hacked into the hotel's computer system to alter both of their extra key cards. She'd gone to her room, after, and changed into jeans and a long-sleeved black t-shirt. Gathered a few items. Put on black running shoes.

"Fancy," she commented as his fingers zipped across the keyboard. She'd thought she'd have to cat-burglar it into the suite, walking along the ledge running around the building just under the windows.

"Efficient," he said. "Voila. Let's go."

No one was in the foyer. The elevator indicator light still said the ground floor. She didn't trust it. She punched the button to bring the elevator back up. She hoped she'd hear it if it headed back down to pick someone up.

P3 first, kitty corner to her suite.

The key card worked, the lock snicking open as he tapped the it against the card reader.

They both pulled on gloves.

A plaintive yowl greeted them as Maggie turned on the overhead lights and Simon shut the door.

A dainty cream cat with a dark gray tail, legs, and face mask, wearing a diamond- and aquamarine- studded collar, stared up at her with vibrant aqua eyes.

So that's how Andreevich blew his cash. Quite the bit of jewelry around the cat's neck.

The cat wove a figure eight around her legs, yowling stridently to be picked up. Not a bit shy. Maggie bent down and the cat leaped into her arms. Her fur was soft as mink, plush and thick. Maggie buried her face into that fur, inhaled. Clean and dry. Cats never smelled like their mouths, though they were covered in cat spit.

"Did you want to do anything besides steal the cat?" Simon asked. "Because we shouldn't dawdle."

"There should be a cat carrier somewhere," she said. "Can you find it? And maybe some cat food."

Simon headed to the bedroom as she cuddled the cat, who was now loudly purring, a deep throated rumble that made her whole tiny body quiver. Maggie could never have hurt this creature.

"I'm sure that cat eats sushi-grade tuna, not mere cat kibble," Simon said from the bedroom. "Aha! Found the carrier and some cans of food."

The front door lock snicked open.

She heard the click, even over the cat's purr next to her ear.

Like she hadn't heard the elevator ping, with the cat's yowling.

She turned even as the door opened.

Andreevich.

Shit shit shit.

Holding the cat with her left hand, she reached for her gun, didn't even think twice, and shot him, even as he opened his mouth to say something.

Then shot the two bodyguards as they pushed to get in the suite, tripping over their employer's dying body.

Good thing Andreevich was dead, because he never had to realize how bad his guards were.

"Bring the carrier," she called, but Simon was already there, carrier in hand, staring at the bodies.

He handed it to her, and she carried it and the cat to the living room table, coaxing the cat inside the carrier. She went in easily, turned once, then curled up. Maggie left the carrier on the table.

"You weren't supposed to kill Andreevich," Simon said.

"What was I supposed to do? Let him kill *us*? Because that's what was going to happen." She dragged Andreevich's body into the suite, far enough she could fit in the bodyguards as well without trailing blood across the entire suite. The carpet was nice. She hated to ruin even a bit of it.

"I have sedatives!" He brandished his gun.

"What, in the bullets?"

"It's a dart pistol. Used for wild animals."

"Maybe you should've told me. Grab the other guard, okay?" she said, yanking on the wrists of the first, piling him next to Andreevich. Simon deposited the second guard next to the other bodies.

"Get the cat," she said. "We'll go to my suite."

———

She was crazy, Simon thought, following Maggie, carrying the cat into her suite. Certifiable. There was no way to fix this, none. They'd both gone against the express wishes of their employers.

She shut the door, leaned up against it. "We gotta go. We're in so much trouble." Her beautiful eyes were twilight flecked with blood moon amber.

He dropped the cat carrier onto the floor and grabbed her, crushing her against him. "You insane woman."

She jumped up, wrapped her legs around his waist, dragged his head to hers, kissed him so hard their teeth clicked. "Wipe your room, I'll take care of mine, we'll go."

"Where?"

"Sun, snow, city?" she asked. "I don't care, as long as it's with you. And our new cat."

She kissed him, a promise of their life to come.

WINNING THE PLAYA REAL BLUFFS HOLIDAY HOP

GWEN LEANED back in her leather gaming chair, the combination of pads and mesh supporting her muscular frame. That butt ugly chair was worth every penny. She'd been coding for the last five hours and nary a twinge in her back.

She stretched, stood up, then tugged open the navy linen curtains behind her monitor, letting in the mid afternoon winter sunlight. She placed her palm against the glass panes. Cool, but not too cold. She braced to yank the window up, tensing her core, protecting her back. The original double hung window, nearly one hundred years old, sometimes swelled and got stuck, especially in the winter.

It opened easily today. Briny ocean air tickled her nose. She didn't have an ocean view from her office window—Jack Jamieson's McMansion next door blocked it—but she still got the breeze off the Pacific.

Winter in coastal Southern California. Gwen wouldn't trade it for anything.

And even if agony in her lower back kept her in bed for the next day, working all morning and early afternoon would have been worth it.

If she won.

She popped three ibuprofen from the bottle in the wire basket on her desk just in case, washing them down with the dregs of room temperature coffee.

No need to tempt fate. She'd overdid it hiking in the Santa Monica mountains last weekend, and spent the next day in bed, barely able to move. Ibuprofen was her friend, though it just took off the edge.

A car accident over Labor Day when she was eleven years old had put her in the hospital for months. She was lucky she could walk, let alone hike or rock climb or bicycle, all the things she'd insisted on being able to do as she grew up.

But that Christmas after the accident—that was the first time she walked again, determinedly clutching the arms of a walker. She marveled at the Christmas lights that transformed her childhood neighborhood of nondescript 1950s tract homes just outside Phoenix into a desert winter wonderland.

Best Christmas *ever*.

Since then, she reached for that sense of wonder every Christmas.

So today? Push it to eleven, baby. Or fifteen. Heck, thirty. Twist that dial UP. Her house would have the best light show ever. Way beyond what she'd ever seen before, in any viral video, and she did her research. She was nothing if not diligent. And determined.

She *would* win the Playa Real Bluffs Holiday Hop decoration competition.

She would beat Jack Jamieson.

It didn't matter she had the smallest house in the Playa Real Bluffs neighborhood: one of the two remaining Spanish bungalows on her block, on the bluff above the beach. Just her and Mrs McGinnes, the long-retired high school chemistry teacher, had tiny old houses.

Mrs McGinnes, a tall rangy woman, bought her home when she started teaching Chemistry and Biology at Playa Real high school in the late 70s, when a teacher could afford a beach cottage.

Gwen bought her bungalow ten years ago, using the signing

bonus from her first job at Charis Games as the down payment plus. Best thing she'd gotten out of that job. She was freelance now.

The rest of the original beach homes up on the bluff had been torn down over the years, making way for a steady stream of trendy McMansions crammed onto tiny lots.

Some were built without as much care as they should've been. Five years ago to the day, the Parkersons' house exploded and slid down the bluff. Conjecture was a small earthquake disrupted the gas line.

But folks still bought up the prime land and built on it, using every square inch they could.

Like Jamieson's modern monstrosity. Three cantilevered concrete blocks with floor to ceiling glass windows on the top two floors, it loomed over the adjacent Mediterranean and Coastal style mansions.

Blocked her ocean view.

Butt ugly piece of architecture.

Which he *paid* to have someone decorate for the holidays. God, he was insufferable.

Men like him were the reason she was freelance. Taking all the credit for what someone else did.

He'd won the Hop last year, with an extravagant display of lights, animatronic reindeer, Santa, and a whole platoon of snowmen, with a snow machine sending fake snowflakes into the air from the roof of his three story house.

Someone said he was best friends with a Disney Imagineer.

Gwen believed it. The display *was* professional.

His workmen took all the street parking the past week, finishing up his display. Left nails and broken boards in the street. Pushed the noise ordinance, cranking up their power tools at 7:00:01 a.m. and not turning them off until 4:49:50 p.m.

Yes, she'd clocked it once.

She suspected that lost ten seconds was a mistake. Bet someone got chewed out for that, Mr Imperious yelling at them.

Though to be fair, she'd never heard him raise his voice once. And their houses were touching distance apart.

Regardless, she'd had to park two blocks over, just before the road wound down to the beach below, whenever she left the house for errands. Parking was at a premium in their tiny neighborhood. Most people respected that, even though technically anyone could park anywhere on the street, residents had "their" spots in front of their homes.

She gritted her teeth just thinking about it. About *him*.

Gwen's display was lights-only, but she programmed the display to re-tell the story of the Grinch using all Star Wars characters, incorporating lights, voice overs, and music. She'd been working on it for three months, late at night, after finishing her contracted work. And now, two weeks before Christmas, just under the neighborhood deadline, she was done.

If she won, she was hoping to spin creating similar displays (with generic characters, of course: she didn't want to catch the attention of the Mouse) into a side gig.

Yes, she was fully aware of the irony. Hiring out her expertise, after she'd bitched about Jamieson hiring folks.

She needed the cash. He didn't.

Sunset and she'd turn on her display.

Tonight, all the neighbors would walk the neighborhood, drinking cocoa or eggnog, checking out all the displays, and texting their votes to Mrs McGinnes at the end of the evening. Just as they did every year for the Playa Real Bluffs Holiday Hop.

Mrs McGinnes would tally the votes and announce the winner the next day.

What did they win? Nada but bragging rights. But that wasn't the point.

Winning was.

Bonkers, her bony old tabby cat, bumped her head against Gwen's leg, purring. Time for lunch, for both of them.

———

Mrs McGinnes had invited Gwen over for a pre-Hop libation. Gwen had accepted. She liked the no-nonsense older woman, still robust in her early seventies. When Gwen had first moved to Playa Real, she'd seen Mrs McGinnes bike to and from the beach, towing her elderly Labrador Hollyberry in a kiddie trailer up and down the hundred and fifty foot elevation change. Gwen didn't doubt Mrs McGinnes could still bike that if she'd gotten another dog after Holly.

Rumor had it she'd retired early from teaching rather than being fired for being too hard on the students. Gwen just thought Mrs McGinnes didn't take any crap from anyone, and that probably pissed off some (male) administrators.

Gwen would have a quick drink, then go home and turn on her lights.

Let the world see her truly amazing spectacular display. Pew, pew!

And choose *her* as the winner.

Although Mrs McGinnes oversaw the Playa Real Bluffs Holiday Hop, she kept her own decorations simple. White icicle lights just under the roofline accentuated the boxy shape of her bungalow while highlighting the glossy blue roof tiles. A family of wire-and-light deer browsed between the fragrant native sages and blue-flowered, glossy-leaved evergreen California lilacs that filled the postage stamp sized front yard. Two potted rosemary bushes, shaped like Christmas trees, twinkled on either side of the solid wood door with its iron grilled Prohibition window.

That was it. Probably took all of an hour or two to set up.

Gwen loved the deer. The whole house and yard projected serenity, compared to the frenetic, kinetic displays on either homes...hers included.

Maybe...maybe next year, she could tone things down.

Nah.

Gwen picked her way along the flagstone path up to Mrs

McGinnes' front door. She normally wore jeans, t-shirts, and sneakers, but had gotten dressed up for the Hop, donning her only little black dress, a classic fit and flare number with a fitted velvet bodice and a full skirt that looked best with the high heeled pumps she never wore otherwise. The skinny stiletto heels just begged to get caught in sidewalk cracks. Or in between flagstones.

So she didn't even notice Jack Jamieson on the saltillo-tiled porch, his fist raised to knock on the door, until she stepped up onto the porch as well.

He'd dressed up, too. A dark suit hugged his muscular body. The crisp white shirt under it just highlighted his surfer's tan. He wore black leather driving moccasins, much more practical than her stilettos. His sun-bleached blond hair was neatly trimmed. He smelled like honey and pinecones, and his smile lit the twilight touched porch.

Her gut twisted. Mrs McGinnes invited him, too?

"Hi, Gwen," he said.

"Jamieson."

"Get your house all done?"

"Sure did. Saw yours has been done for a few days."

"Yep. Didn't want to wait to the last minute, you know?" His smile grew broader.

Asshole.

"I'm sure you *paid* them well to finish up on time."

The door opened.

"Come in, you two! Happy Holidays." Mrs McGinnes ushered them in. She had smudges of flour on her cheekbone and on her red gingham apron. Appliquéd sloths wearing jaunty Santa hats decorated the bodice of the apron. Her long gray hair was tied back in a long ponytail.

"I made some special cookies, just for the two of you. My version of Italian wedding cookies, but with candied persimmon," said Mrs McGinnes. "I'm lucky enough to have a persimmon tree in my little backyard. I have to come up with ways to use all the fruit."

"Sounds wonderful," Jamieson said.

"Start off with a bit of eggnog to go with? I made it myself. I blend in persimmons right before serving. Cuts down on the calories, you know. I don't have to use as much sugar when I'm making it."

Gwen nodded. Cookies and eggnog. She was going to have to do a run tomorrow, aching back or not. No matter if the persimmons really made a difference with the calorie count.

"Sit, sit!" Mrs McGinnes gestured to the plush natural cotton slip-covered sofa in her living room. Her house was the mirror image of Gwen's: a nice sized living room to the left of the front door, a small dining room to the right, with the kitchen beyond it to the right, and a hallway to the bedrooms and bathroom off the left of the dining room. It was decorated in a spare, updated farmhouse-chic style, with bright white plastered walls and mellow golden oak floors. It smelled like warm cinnamon and apples and pine.

Two small plates with three powder-sugar-covered cookies each were already on the reclaimed wood coffee table in front of the sofa, along with two mugs of eggnog, sprinkled with nutmeg. "I have to get changed for the Hop. Won't take me more than a minute, so you two just dig in!"

Jamieson sprawled onto the couch, man-spreading over a cushion and a half, in front of one place setting. He patted the remainder of the center cushion. Jerk.

She perched on the edge of the couch, opposite end, then sighed and sat fully on the couch. Her back couldn't take it, otherwise.

He smirked. "Cheers," he said, lifting his glass of eggnog and tilting it in a toast in her direction. "Come on. If you don't drink it, you'll hurt Mrs McGinnes' feelings."

"I think she's tougher than that." But Gwen lifted her glass and took a sip.

Nice. The nutmeg was a bit bitter, but the eggnog was creamy and rich, with a buttery caramel fruity flavor. She drank nearly half the mug, letting the creaminess coat her mouth. She never cooked or made anything this decadent for herself.

"It's really good," Jamieson said, setting his mug down. He

grabbed a cookie. "My aunt used to make cookies like these for Christmas. I haven't had them in years." He popped the whole cookie into his mouth.

Gwen nibbled on a cookie. The powdered sugar melted on her tongue, followed by the flaky cookie itself.

Again, a slight hint of bitterness.

"Jack?" Gwen said. "Do you think these taste a little off?"

He swigged some more eggnog. "I—" He shook his head like an irritated dog. "I think my tongue ish nub. 'N can't feel my facsh."

Jack slumped on the couch, taking two full cushions.

Her right knee was resting against his left knee, the skirt of her dress hiked up to mid thigh. She'd slid, but the velvet fabric, sticky against the nubby cotton of the slipcover, hadn't.

When had she slid?

Gwen looked at Jack. "You're blurry. Actually, you're two. Two of you." Her cookie fell in slow motion, hitting the oak floor with a resonating BOOM, powdered sugar and crumbs scattering in concentric circles.

Shoes thudded against the wood floor. Mrs McGinnes stood on the either side of the coffee table, hands on her hips.

She was dressed like Santa. Or a brawny Mrs Santa. Or an elf. Gwen's brain just wouldn't work.

McGinnes wore red fuzzy jacket, trimmed with white fluff at the cuffs and collar, and black leggings tucked into worn black Doc Martens.

Whatever that outfit made her.

Besides a poisoning *psychopath*.

"Oh, wonderful. That didn't take nearly as long as I thought it would."

"Wha di oo FEED ush?" Jamieson croaked.

"Just something to give you two a chance to ponder your choices. And make some decisions about what you're going to do next."

"Hop shtrartsh soon," Gwen said.

"No one will miss either of you. That's part of the problem, you see." McGinnes shook her head. "Really, it's the whole neighborhood. It used to be so different. Cozier. People cared about each other. Now just a handful know the people just a couple doors down, let alone everyone in the neighborhood.

"But you two are the worst.

"Everything about this Hop—neighborliness, the joy of the season, all that—has been perverted into a crass display of ego—" McGinnes wagged a finger at Gwen—"and excess." She nodded at Jack.

Gwen didn't think it was very Christmas-like to POISON someone, either. But she couldn't form the words. Jack seemed to agree, though all he could do was glare with glazed blue eyes at McGinnes.

"Now, I do have an antidote. But I don't know if either of you deserve it." McGinnes collected the plates and the mugs. "The first time I had to go this far, oh, it was fifteen or twenty years ago, I'm sorry to say they couldn't convince me. What a mess I had to deal with, after. Are you *Breaking Bad* fans? They did a good job with addressing the complications of dealing with a dead body in that show. Of course, I didn't use a cast iron tub. Regardless, such a wonderful show, don't you think? I'm going to get these dishes cleaned up."

Gwen couldn't even move to watch McGinnes bustle to the kitchen. She could *hear* her, the thud thud thud of her Docs echoing off the plaster walls, then the clatter of plates and the chug of the garbage disposal.

"Gwe?"

"'ere."

"She'sh nutsh."

"Yeah."

"Sh' want?"

Gwen didn't know. What could they do, to placate McGinnes? Why would McGinnes believe anything they said (or slurred) to her? Promises to get along and be best buddies?

Gwen didn't want to *die*. Her fingertips were totally numb. She couldn't feel the rough cotton of the slipcover under her palms, just pressure.

And she couldn't move.

She'd swear to anything for the damn antidote.

If there even was an antidote.

Thud thud thud. McGinnes was back in front of them.

"So. Have you two thought about this?" She peered at them. "Ah. Cat's got your tongues. This is very simple. One of you gets to leave here. The other doesn't.

"And don't forget I was a chemistry teacher. If the survivor says a word of this to anyone, I'll blow your house sky high. Remember the Parkersons?" She chuckled. "I'll assume that's a yes."

Oh god. The house that toppled down the cliff.

That was no earthquake. No faulty gas line.

McGinnes regarded them. "Your turn, Jack. Who gets to leave—you or Gwen? Blink once for Jack, twice for Gwen."

Gwen couldn't turn her head to look at him.

"Hmm. Interesting. Gwen? I'm rooting for you, girl. I think you have a better shot at changing. Who gets to leave? You or Jack?"

What did McGinnes watch besides *Breaking Bad*? *Saw* or some other torture porn crap?

Fuck you, lady.

Gwen never gave up. Not once in her life.

And not now.

Gwen blinked three times, hard. No mistake.

McGinnes clapped her hands together. "Oh, you two are the best! If I didn't know any better, I'd've said you two were suited for each other. But I'm serious. Only one of you gets to leave. Jack?"

Oh, Gwen wished she could move, just the tiniest bit, to see him.

"Gwen?"

Fuck *you*. A tear trickled down her cheek, and she couldn't even wipe it off.

Gwen didn't want to die. But she couldn't condemn someone else.

She blinked once, firmly, squeezing out one more tear.

"Ah." McGinnes sat down in the armchair kitty corner to the couch. "Maybe there's hope."

"Mmph?" Jack grunted.

"You both ingested a good amount of persimmon. Hachiya persimmon. *Unripe* Hachiya persimmon. Mixed with a concoction of my own creation to extend the effects of eating, well, unripe persimmons." She waved her hand. "It can cause tingling, then loss of sensation. You'll be *fine*, in a couple of hours. And Jack, so you know, Gwen blinked once. And Jack blinked twice. The first time you both blinked three times."

Gwen narrowed her eyes.

Then realized she *could* narrow her eyes.

"'oo," she spat, "are a ver' bad pershon!"

McGinnes smiled. "Yes. But I am a very, *very* effective teacher." She paused, then smiled brightly. "And I can still blow up your house. So don't say a damn thing to anyone."

————

Five hours later, they could both move enough to stand up and walk, albeit Gwen was so stiff she was going to have to pop more ibuprofen and sleep with her heating pad.

McGinnes let them use her bathroom. Gwen inspected the toilet to make sure it wasn't booby trapped.

Jack walked Gwen home. The street was empty and quiet. The next day was a workday. They stopped in front of his home first.

The snow machine had kicked in, blowing out swirls of snowflakes, dotting their faces with quickly melting dabs of fake snow.

The reindeer tossed their heads and stamped their hooves.

The snowman doffed his black silk hat. "Haaa-ppy Birthday!" it said in a bright voice. "Isn't it wonderful to be alive?"

"I had it set on a timer," Jack said.

Gwen swallowed. "Mine wasn't." Her house was dark, on the other side of Jack's. She'd wanted to turn it on herself. Hands on, the whole way.

"I don't care who wins."

She believed him. Despite herself, she believed him.

Gwen hugged herself. "I sorta do. Part of me. But in the big scheme, not really. Not anymore. And all this?" she gestured at his house. "It really is lovely."

"I'm going to tell the police about this. What she did to us."

"She's a pillar of the community. And I think the chief was one of her students." And the Parkersons' house....Gwen didn't have to say it.

"She didn't blow up their house, Gwen. I researched all of that before I built my place. They built too close to the edge of the cliff, that's all. It can happen."

"I think, in her own way, then, she meant well. Tough love."

"I'll let it go if you want me too."

Gwen looked past his house, to her small dark house. *Her* house. She earned it. She wasn't going to jeopardize it. "I think I do."

He reached for her hand tentatively. She let him hold it, her own hand still, then twined her fingers with his. Yeah, they were okay. None worse for the wear. But she *had* thought she was dying. That they both would die.

Short term, they were fine.

Someday, she would get payback.

On her own terms.

When it really mattered, Gwen always got what she worked for.

McGinnes wouldn't get the chance to terrorize anyone again.

"Show me what you made?" Jack asked. "I really want to see it. I'm good with money, but I wish I had your creativity. I've always been in awe of you."

"Okay, that's a bit much," she laughed. "But yeah. Come on.

"I'll show you the most abso-fucking-lutely amazing light show you will *ever* see."

ABOUT THE AUTHOR

Since graduating from West Point, Stephannie Tallent has served in the Army as a Military Intelligence officer during Desert Storm, gotten a Zoology degree, went to vet school, worked as a small animal veterinarian, and designed and published knitting patterns and books.

Throughout all that she's always wanted to be a writer, and she's finally put all her type A, soft-spoken, invisible middle-aged woman focus on that goal, writing everything from fantasy to science fiction, mysteries and romance.

She has sold stories to **Pulphouse Magazine** and the **WMG Holiday Spectacular**.

www.stephannietallent.com

Sign up for Stephannie's newsletter!
https://www.stephannietallent.com/subscribe/

ALSO BY STEPHANNIE TALLENT

Short Story Collections

Gates of Wonder

The Chronicles of Dinah Lee Wright Vol 1

The Chronicles of Dinah Lee Wright Vol 2

Gratitude of the Ocean: Jolene Tomberlin Series

The Serpent in the Shallows: Jolene Tomberlin Series

The Monkey's Journal

The Kaleidoscope Jaguars of the Jungles of Mexicatl

The Mermaid of Ellis Prime

The Alchemy of Science and Mystery

One Plus One Equals More (mystery/crime)

A Snowman Made of Sand (romance)

KnitWitch (fantasy and knitting patterns)

www.ingramcontent.com/pod-product-compliance
Lightning Source LLC
Chambersburg PA
CBHW010559170726
48285CB00011B/2975